MARY ON KENNEDY

Book #1 of the Insurance Man's Kids Series

DONNA IVEY-BRYANT

DONNA IVEY-BRYANT

This is a book of fiction, inspired by a true story.

Author's website: www.Donnaivey-bryant.com

:

DEDICATION

This book is dedicated, in loving memory, to my parents

Mary Alice & Jackson Ivey

I

Sheep In Wolves Clothing

Contents

ACKNOWLEDGMENTS

Thanks

To my husband, Willie, for encouraging me to pursue my passion—writing.

My sister, Bernice, for her support and editing—from the beginning to end.

Rogina, for being a friend and encouraging me to get my work published.

Sonya, for being a friend and my sounding board.

I've never desired great fortune or fame
Only to be treated with dignity and basically the same

All my life I've trusted in the Lord
As a result, all my needs I was able to afford

Yes, God show has been good to me
I'm deeply rooted, just like an old tree

My reputation and word is good
Throughout my neighborhood

I suppose that's why they call me
Mary on Kennedy

The Perfect Mother's Day Gift

For being your mom, I thank God
He has given me a remarkable job
The gift I desire, you can't buy in a store
It's the gift that every mother prays for

Please keep your life together
Don't just settle-I expect each generation to be better
You have sisters & brothers
You really should help each other

I've been accused of loving some of you too strong
But don't be jealous if you felt all alone or as if you didn't
belong
I was only giving special attention to the ones who were going
wrong

Remember all of the scolding
It was all part of the molding
If I seemed to push you harder
It's because I knew you could go farther

From my mistakes you must learn
Just strive to do better when it's your turn
You must realize, now that you're an adult
Any mistakes you make are your fault
Please try to minimize your mistakes
Because they will keep me awake

When you don't know what I want and you just want to shout
Ask the one who thinks she knows everything-she's figured me
out

You all are decedents of a people who survived with very little
means
But never lost sight of their dreams

So go around or get over whatever holds you back
Do you think it was easy for me and Jack?
 I've been a mother for 65 plus years!
Thank you for the many gifts throughout the years
Especially for the perfect gift-**more joy than tears**
And know that each one of you gives my spirit a lift
And I truly thank God for my nine gifts

Colors from Di

PROLOGUE

I WAS A DADDY'S girl and my daddy was a funny and caring man. His passing left a void in my heart, but the memories and my mother's spirited presence aided me in dealing with his absence. In point of fact, my dad's passing closed the tunnel vision that I had exclusively for him, and allowed me to meet the strong woman that kept her vow (56 years) and never parted—until his last breath—my mother (Mary Alice Ivey).

Our mother, at age 86, had a massive stroke, which left her in need of care and the odds of a 100% recovery from such a colossal stroke was not in her favor, given her other pre-existing maladies. As a result, my sister Bernice and I decided we were going to care for her at my home. The second floor of my quad level home was remodeled into an en-suite bedroom to comfortably accommodate our mother's need for privacy and dignity.

My actions sound selfless, but they were totally selfish. It was my last chance to have her undivided attention, and yes the 7th child out of 9 had issues. Ultimately, I wanted to give her what she had given me since my birth—undying love and assistance.

We spent every day talking, laughing, and crying; but there were absolutely no tears of sorrow.

DONNA IVEY-BRYANT

1: MAW! CAN YOU HEAR ME?

"HELLO, I'M DR. BALASUB, I am Mary Alice's neurologist," echoed a short man, with dark skin tone and straight, jet black hair, seemingly of Indian descent. "She has suffered a massive ischemic stroke and the next 48 hours will determine the severity of the damage to her brain."

He walked over to a portable computer terminal that a nurse had pushed into the room, he tapped the screen and a 3-D replica of a brain appeared. "This is a picture of Mary Alice's brain, it is swelling at a massive rate. The family must decide if you want me to perform a hemicraniectomy." Dr. Balasub tapped the computer screen and a picture of a skull appeared. "The brain is encased by the walls of the bony skull. We are not able to determine if the brain will stop swelling beyond the confines of her skull. But if the swelling does not stop, the result is brain death." Dr. Balasub tapped the computer screen once again, and an image of a human skull with a round section removed from the left, front side revealing the brain. "The hemicraniectomy is a surgical procedure, where I will remove a portion of the skull, as you can see here on the screen, it will allow room for the brain to expand."

The eight children circling their mother's bed, and staring like lost lambs, were totally flabbergasted by the 5 minute crash course on brain surgery. Reba was the first to speak, "How much time do we have to decide?"

"Unfortunately, time is not a luxury that your mother can afford, the decision must be made immediately," replied Dr. Balasub.

Reba's heart (driven by her inner child), and brain (controlled by the mature adult) were at battle "What would mom want us to do?" Reba thought while silently praying for guidance. She stood, and said to her heavy laden sisters and brothers, "I believe this type of surgery would be fatal. If God is ready for her, he will surely take her, with or without this procedure." Bernice, Reba's older sister, immediately agreed as did the others, and the doctor vanished as quickly as he had appeared.

Reba leaned beside her mother, and whispered in a childlike voice, "Maw! Maw! Can you hear me? It's your baby!" Hoping her mother would hear her humble cry, and awaken from her stroke sedated slumber.

Mary Alice clearly recognized the voice of her child, and instinctively reacted to her child's distressful cry, as she had every night of her child's first 9 years. She hurdled from her bed, and headed for her daughter's room. She motioned to open the door, but realized she was not at her daughter's bedroom door, but at the front door, and someone was on the other side knocking. She looked through the peep hole, but the reflective light was too bright, so she reached for the door handle to open the door, but her child's voice began screaming again, "Maw! Maw! It's Reba, your baby. Can you hear me, Maw? I need you." She gestured to turn around, and go comfort her child, but she couldn't move. She thought, "I'm having that dream again, where I think I'm awake and I can't move. I just need to move my finger to wake myself up."

"I felt it Maw! I felt you move your finger!" Reba said joyously. "We're all here—Bernice, Sara, Bay, Nate, Ronnie, Dawn and Dwan, so don't worry, you will be ok."

Mary Alice could hear her daughter talking, but the words were faint, her child sounded as though she were traveling through a tunnel and moving farther and farther away. She willed her body to move, she wanted to talk, but her body would not cooperate. Suddenly other voices chimed in, but these voices were loud and clear, but they were speaking in a language that she didn't understand, then she realized she was at the front door again and these voices where coming from the opposite side. She opened the door and a light, as bright as the sun, coupled with a soft, fragrant breeze filled the room. She had to close her eyes, so as not to be blinded, as three men in robes, as white and radiant as the light that preceded them, entered into the room. They didn't utter a word as one stood on her right side, one stood on her left, and the other stood in front of her. She felt an inexpressible blanket of serenity that covered her very being. The one on the right and on the left gently held her arm and braced her back, as they leaned her backwards into a warm body of water, and they remained by her side, still as Sovereign Guards, and she rested.

Mary Alice's children warily remained by her side, never leaving her completely alone for a moment. Twenty-seven hours later, the neurologist entered the room. "Hello I am Dr. Balasub, Mary Alice's Neurologist. Her Head CT scan results confirm the brain has stabilized and she should be awakening soon. However, Mary Alice has sustained severe damage to the right side of her brain. This side of the brain controls her left side and upon completing her stay at the hospital, she will require rehabilitation. The rehabilitation is crucial because the brain will forget that side of the body, if the range of motion is not restored. I will continue to check on her periodically, but at this point my services are no longer necessary. However, if you should have any questions, do not hesitate to call me. He touched her shoulder, and said, "get well soon Mary Alice," then nodded in the direction of the family, smiled, and left the room.

After 15 days in the hospital, she was transferred to a rehabilitation facility for 100 days. The family continued their vigil over their mother, thereby ensuring that her medical care was exemplary. However, after about 5 days at the hospital, the eight-children-vigil had dwindle down to two. Even though the world had stopped for Mary Alice's children, the rest of the world continued business as usual. Consequently, some of her children had to return to the demands of their everyday lives. Fortunately, her daughter, Reba, was self-employed and modified her schedule to be with her mom. And, in spite of her full-time work schedule, Bernice (Mary Alice's favorite child) traveled thirty additional miles after work every day to see about her mother.

The time spent at the rehabilitation facility was rigorous and totally exhausting for Mary Alice. But she made it through all the therapy sessions, and was released to go home. The social worker and nurses at the rehabilitation facility trained Bernice, and Reba so that they would be prepared for the demanding responsibilities vital for the care of a stroke patient. Finally, the day arrived and she was released into the care of her family and taken to Reba's home.

2: DO YOU REMEMBER?

AS TIME PASSED AND MARY ALICE grew stronger, she regained her sense of humor, and a desire to talk to people of her choice—specifically, her daughter's Bernice and Reba. Often times when her therapists, or even some friends and relatives came to visit, she wouldn't utter a single word, until they left. Then she would say, "He didn't know what he was doing," or "that child aint never had nothing worth-while to say." All Reba could do was laugh, and shake her head.

One day during a routine memory exercise, Reba asked, "Ma can you recall your childhood?"

"Yes," Mary Alice replied matter-of-factly, "I can remember back when I was a child going to school."

"Really, what do you remember about going to school?"

"Well I remember when my dad decided the boys were wasting time with schooling, and would be more useful contributing to the household, so he pulled them out of school after they were able to read, and sign their names."

Reba knew this to be accurate because her mom told her that story, before she had the stroke.

"Well, do you remember me asking about your childhood, growing up in Alabama, your single years in Ohio, and then marrying daddy and moving to Indiana? No matter how many times I asked, you would give me the same answer, 'Child I could write a book and it would be a best seller,'" Reba said imitating her mother.

They both burst into laughter.

"Yes, I remember."

"Well, I would like to know all the family secrets that you would never tell me. I mean that's part of my history."

"It's getting late, what time is it getting to be? Bernice should be here soon." Mary Alice said looking toward the front door, deliberately changing the subject.

"Maw, your own children don't know very much about your life before you married dad and started a family of your own. I swear the Upshaw's can keep a secret."

"I suppose I can share our secrets with you." Mary Alice said in a defeated voice, yet still staring in the direction of the front door, wishing Bernice would enter so she could change the subject. "Since for all intents and purposes most of my brothers and sisters have gone on to glory," Mary Alice chuckled, then her smile inverted to a sad face "but don't say you swear about nothing—God don't like that."

"Okay, sorry Ma. And its 9a.m., Bernice don't get off work for another five hours," Reba said so her mom could stop staring at the door.

"*It's just you and your baby, so get to talking,*" Reba said to herself.

3: MY SHIP HAS FINALLY COME

IN 1942, A GROUP OF SILENT generation Negro men and women from Pittsview, Alabama, ranging in ages from 15 to 20 years, were talking about migrating up north to East Chicago, IN. The good news had traveled 821 miles to a dirt road off highway 241. The good news was that the oil refineries and steel mills in Indiana were hiring Negroes.

"A group of us called ourselves the Pittsview peeps. It was me, Jackson (Moon) Ivey, William (Son) Ivey, Linda Upshaw, William (Pappy) Glen, and some others, whose names escape me right now. Well, we met at the Frog Pond, every Saturday, to discuss our plan to move up North. The plan was to send four lookout men with the mission of finding a job, a place to live; and to honor an oath to help the next relative coming up north. No matter what, we was gone stick together."

"Well my plans changed when I received a letter from my brother, Willie. He invited me to come to Cincinnati to visit him for the summer. There would be no more dreaming for me, under that weeping willow tree, about one day leaving the south and having a fabulous life up North. My brother had been gone around about 2 years, he was a soldier in World War II, and I missed him something terribly. I especially missed how we pretended to travel as he swept the dirt to form walkways to the front porch stairs of our house. He would sweep a lane on his left from south to northeast, then jump inside of it and sing and sway his shoulders, as if dancing with the broom. 'I'm in New York!' He'd shout. Then he would turn and sweep Midwest and say, 'Look out Mary Alice cuz ole Willie's in Chicago!' I would laugh and jump in each lane he created, and dance along while grabbing the broom with him and swaying my hips, and shouting 'I'm right there with you Bruh Shaw.' By the time we finished our chores, we had dream-traveled to every major city in the United States."

"Now, my only problem was getting permission, from my mom and dad, to go up North to visit Bruh Shaw. I couldn't just up and leave like folks do today, nope that would've been disrespectful. Plus, my Mom and Dad had decided, long ago, on what I was going to do after I graduated from high school. I was to be a dressmaker, because they figured I had a knack for sewing because I always helped my mom with her dressmaking business. She made some of the most beautiful wedding dresses, I have yet to see one more detailed. She was a natural with pearls, and netting, and rosettes. She also made party dresses for the local women. But if truth be told," she chuckled, "I only started helping mom because I didn't want to haul all our clothes down to the brook to wash. So I would get up bright and early on Saturday morning, my dad had to threaten a beating to get my brothers and sisters out of that bed. I would get all the clothes sorted and packed for the 3 mile journey. While I was waiting for the others to get ready, I would go into mom's sewing room and ask her if there was anything I could help her with until the kids got ready. Mom always had something for me to do and always wanted me to try on something she was making." She would tell me the same thing every Saturday, 'Mary Alice, you have a perfect figure and you always look like you're wearing heels because you are so tall.' Mom was so proud that at least one of her children took an interest in sewing, like her. By the time my brothers and sisters were ready, she told them to go on without me because she needed my help. My brothers and sisters would be so mad at me. I'm tellin you, and if looks could kill I would have been a gone girl." Mary Alice laughed out loud as she reminisced. "They had to lug those clothes to the brook without me, but the worst part was lugging them back, wet. From that day forward, my Saturdays were spent with my mom and I learned not only how to sew, but how to dress, run a business and how to negotiate with the white folks."

"Maw, how did your mom manage to have her own business at home back in those days?" Reba asked, *actually wondering if her mom was embellishing the truth, but choosing her words ever so carefully so as not to imply her mom was lying. Because Reba knew, oh so well, that Mary Alice would go completely left, and then answer with a question, 'so Reeebah you callin me a lie? Is that what you sayin?' and give her a look that would make the devil tremble.*

"Well, my mom was working at Miss Janice dress shop in Montgomery. Shortly after my bruh Joe was born, mom got sickly and told her she was gone have to quit, because traveling to town was getting to be too much on her. You see, my mom didn't graduate from high school because most Negroes in the south were farmers, not rocket scientists; a formal education didn't amount to hill of beans, in those days, you understand."

Reba shook her head confirming she was on the same page as her mom.

"There was no denying that sewing was Willie B Upshaw's God given gift, and she was naturally smart, I mean smart as a whip. She could tell you, just from looking at you, the amount of material you would need to make a dress and she didn't need no patterns. And when we delivered the finished wedding gowns to the dress shop in Columbus, they all would be in awe when they saw mom's creation. She would spew out the amount she was due so fast, that those white women would just agree, opposed to allowing their transparent skin to show their embarrassment, over her being able to add those numbers in her head, faster than they could with pen and pad."

"Nah, of course Miss Janice was taking all the credit for all my mom's work, and would have gone out of business without the ideas and talent of my mom. So, Miss Janice sent eight white men to our house, and two weeks later they had built an addition onto our house, and furnished it with everything my mom needed to make those wedding dresses. On the surface, it looked like a good thing, but if she really cared anything for my mom, she would have been trying to get her some medical attention. Hmm, child you got to recognize a wolf dressed in sheep's clothing. You best believe Willie Bee Upshaw was not fooled by her skullduggery, and that sewing room made my mom more money than it did Miss Janice."

Reba noticed that her mom got a tad bit peeved from that memory, so she moved away from that subject by asking, "So ma, how did you manage to go see your brother, Willie?"

Mary Alice's constricted facial expression relaxed, and she said, "Well I remembered that my best friend, Pearl and her sister Nan were moving to Cincinnati, after Pearl and I graduated from Glenville High School. So first, I asked my mom if I could go visit my brother for the summer. My mom knew how much I missed my brother, as did she. Not knowing if she would ever have the chance to see him again, weighed heavy on her mind ever since the day he up and joined the army. Willie wrote letters to mom on the regular, telling her he was doing real good; and he sent money in each letter, instructing her to give it to dad, but he never came back to Pittsview. Now my dad would console my mom by telling her, 'W.B. don't you fret none, long as he keep writing, he doin ok.' My dad was ok because Willie was sending him some money, on the regular." Mary Alice chuckled thinking about her dad.

"So mom told me, 'Mary Alice, it's ok with me, but yah daddy got the last word.' My mom wanted me to check on Willie and she also wanted me to have the experiences associated with traveling. She knew that I was never coming back (just like bruh Shaw), maybe to visit but never to live in the south! Nor did she want me to be subject to the guises of that shyster, Miss Janice!"

"Aww, sookie, sookie, now! Look at Mary Alice, she's still a lil salty with Miss Janice," Reba thought to herself as she laughed within.

"Anyways, after much pondering under the weeping willow tree trying to think of how was I going to get a yes out of my dad, suddenly it hit me, and I knew exactly what I would say to sway him! I jumped up with glee and started swaying my hips and singing 'look out bruh Shaw cuz Mary Alice is comin to Cincinnati!'"

"Mr. Ervin Upshaw," Mary Alice smiled as she proudly said her dad's name, "my dad, considered himself a business man. Busy at mastering how to work smart but not hard. But his father," Mary Alice held her head down in shame, "Shim Upshaw, now he was a son-of-gun, just walked off and left Grandma Shood, her real name was Sarah, and ten kids to just root hog or die pig. Some folks said he traveled from one county to the next preaching the word of God and accepting church offerings as he moved to the next county. My dad was the oldest child and was just about eleven years old when he became the man of the house. He would wake up early in the morning and come back by noon with enough food to feed the entire family. He was not a shy child and had favor when it came to asking for odd jobs to take care of his family.

"On one of his outings, he came upon an unconscious white man (Mr. Joe) whose leg was wedged under a wagon axle and bleeding. My dad used the man's shirt to make a bandage for his leg and hitched a rope across a branch and then tied it to Mr. Joe's horse to lift the carriage and then pulled Mr. Joe from underneath the wagon. He then used the man's horse to get to the nearest farm and asked them to come help. When Mr. Joe recovered and was told about what the lil negro boy had done for him, he was so grateful that he hired my dad to just sit alongside him as he traveled from farm to farm to pick up his rations. Mr. Joe gave Grandma Shood so much food, she had enough to share with others less fortunate. You see, at that time, Mr. Joe was one of the wealthiest farmers in Russell County.

"My dad told me that he's been a business man ever since

he was knee high to a wagon wheel. Not only was he able to take care of his mother and siblings, but he was able to save most of his wages. After his mother died and all his siblings were of age to fend for themselves, he married the prettiest girl in town, (my mom); he bought the big house where his great-great grandma was born on the day her mother heard slavery had ended – June 20, 1865; and he bought a general store on highway 241."

"Now, I say all that, to say this, that night after dad finished eating his supper, he sat in his favorite rocking chair on our front porch (of the big house), where he enjoyed smoking a Camel cigarette while catching an evening breeze. I joined him that evening and as I sat on the step beside his feet, I said, in the humblest tone I could muster up, 'daddy can I please go to Cincinnati, just for the summer to see Willie? Willie said he'd pay my way there and back. Nan and Pearl are moving to Cincinnati, I could ride the train with them. While I'm there, I'm sure to find a job and I can send you money every payday, so as to help out with things at home.' I just sat quietly, as I patiently waited for Mr. Ervin Upshaw, the business man, to calculate how much money he could collect from me, plus what he was already getting from my bruh Willie. It seemed like an eternity, as I watched the sunset and my dad smoke that entire cigarette before he said one word. But when he said, 'Mary Alice when you thinkin bout leavin?' I saw my ship come in, I jumped to my feet and gave him a kiss on the cheek and said, 'Thank you daddy! They leavin next week, Thursday.'

"My dad knew I was never coming back to the south to live, but he was ok with me moving up North, as long as I wrote (and sent him money) on a regular basis."

"I skipped in the house singing and my sis Linda asked, 'Mary Alice, what are you so happy about?' I was performing my victory dance, as I swayed my hips, and raised arms, in opposite directions to a song in my heart, as I sang her the answer, 'I'm goin to Cincinnati, I'm goin to Cincinnati!'"

"Linda frowned and in an angry tone asked, 'how come you

get to go! I'm the oldest?'"

"I didn't stop dancing or singing, as I replied. 'cuz you didn't ask first.'"

At that moment, Linda understood what pastor was screaming about in his sermon when he said, 'Favor ain't fair.'

4: BEING AT THE RIGHT PLACE, AT THE RIGHT TIME

"THAT NEXT FRIDAY, I was in Cincinnati, bruh Shaw met me at the train station and showed me around the town, and introduced me to all his soldier buddies, he said 'This here is my sister, Mary Alice, touch her and yoh momma will have somewhere to go in the mornin,' and they all burst into laughter like that was the funniest thing they had ever heard.

"I found out some time later that they knew he was as serious as World War II. They all laughed, as if he was joking, because he had pre-warned them the week before my arrival." Mary Alice, laughed. "Densale, one of the soldiers, told me Willie called them together, during target practice, and Willie was shooting the target silhouettes in the private areas, then he tells them, 'My sister is comin to town, and if any of you jokers touch her, I promise yoh momma will have to come identify your body at the morgue.' "I suppose he figured, the shooting range was the best place for his comrades to grasp the level of sincerity of his promise, because he also said, 'This is war boys, there will be no dress rehearsals.

"Well, needless to say, I had no trouble with any of those

soldiers, and believe-you-me, I had plenty of suitors." Mary Alice chuckled.

"I remember getting ready for my first date. Private Densale Washington," Mary Alice said slowly and passionately, "asked me to accompany him to the Army annual black tie ball, it was my first formal event! He was 6' tall and muscular. He was easy on the eyes, with his pecan brown skin and dark brown thick hair, thick perfectly arched eyebrows and long eyelashes with big almond shaped brown eyes, high cheekbones and long narrow nose, thin lips and a cleft chin. He was always smiling and showing off his natural straight teeth. If times were different, he could have been a movie star.

Reba thought to herself, *"TMI alert! I don't think I want to hear this story, and where the hell was my daddy?"*

"I called and told my mom I needed a dress, and she made me a dress that fit me like it was poured on me. I was a real head-turner in that dress: It had a strapless lace bodice covered with sequins, beads and rhinestones; it fit like skin down to the hips; and then two long panels of pleated chiffon draped around the back of my lower waist, and then met in the front forming a 'V' at the bottom of the lace bodice, the remaining fabric blended with the skirt of my gown, which was silver charmeuse satin with overlays of silver blue chiffon.

"When my brother saw me in that dress, he said, 'Mary Alice, don't let no man try to trick you. Always have at least enough money to call me if some joker aint acting right. Don't believe everything you hear and only half of what see. These boys gettin with any and every girl that will let them. You save yourself for the right man, one who will work hard and not leave. Cuz if you make your bed hard you gone have to sleep in it.'

"I listened to every word because I knew my brother only wanted the best for me. I enjoyed going out to various social events and in the beginning accepted dates from several gentlemen callers. You see I was living with my brother on the army housing base, so there were more single men than single women. So with that and being a fox, I had more than my fair share of eligible men trying to court me. As a matter-of-fact, Densale, the boy who took me to the Army ball, well he asked my brother's permission to ask me to marry him." Mary Alice said, without reservation.

Reba was distraught by this news and thought, *'What? Are you kidding me? I almost wasn't born? Oh my God! Where was my daddy, I mean really?'* But she had to remain calm, so as not to risk her mom shutting down because she couldn't handle the truth.

"Densale told me, 'When I asked your brother for permission to ask you to marry me, his facial expression changed for the worse as he swiftly stepped forward, and up close into my personal space, and he says, 'What's the rush Densale?' I says, 'Shaw, it aint what you thinkin, man! I got my orders, I'm shippin out in 48 hours. I figured if I don't make it back, Mary Alice could receive the widow benefits. Aint no sense in me dying for nothin.'

'And if you return, unscathed, what then, Private Washington?' asked Bruh Shaw.

'By this time I was all nervous and tongue tied, cuz I knew how crazy he could get, so all I could get out was, Then I suppose um, I suppose… I didn't think that far ahead.'

'In a deep, slow voice, and meaner than a drill sergeant, he said, 'Well let me do yoh stinkin, thinkin for you, soldier. Don't dangle that bullshit in my sister's face. She don't need to be no widow, and she show don't need to be your wife when you get back. You are dismissed, soldier.'

"'I took advantage of the opportunity, and left,' Densale said in a frightened voice.'"

Reba smiled and said to herself, *"Bruh Shaw is officially my favorite Uncle."*

"Now Densale's front-line-proposal wasn't uncommon during war times, plenty of resourceful women used the soldiers as their cash cow, some of them was receiving multiple checks," Mary Alice said in a nonchalant tone. "But I told Densale that I really wasn't interested in a serious relationship, at this time in my life, and marriage was as serious as it gets."

In a proud and sincere voice, she said, "I thank God, I never had to resort to such things, but I do understand why they did it—the United States were united against colored folks back in those days. Even so, I needed to see and experience the world before settling down and having children, and I wasn't going to do anything that could possibly land me back in Pittsview, Alabama."

"The Pittsview, Alabama where you left my daddy! While you're livin la viva loca? Adios mío! Dónde estás Padre?" Reba exclaimed to herself.

Mary Alice asked, "Did I ever tell you how I got that job?"

"Yes, you told me your girlfriend, Pearl, was applying for the job, and you were just going along to keep her company."

"Yes, that's correct. We had only been in Cincinnati four days, I was still on vacation. But Pearl needed to find a job right away, because they only had enough money saved to cover one month's rent."

"I don't recall ever meeting Miss Pearl, how did she look?"

"Well," Mary Alice squinted as she spoke, as if the memory of her friend was almost too far away to see, "She was short, a lil over five feet, with a small upper body and tiny waist, wide hips and big legs. She had a flawless dark chocolate complexion, a widow's peak, narrow eyes that always looked like she was sleepy, and full lips. Her hair went past her shoulders when straightened, but she always wore it pinned back. She always wore a hat or a scarf because her hair was so thick that it would sweat out a press & curl after a few hours." She smiled and gazed ahead, as if she had summoned up her long gone friend into the room.

"Pearl told me 'Mair Alice,' "That's what she called me, poor thang couldn't pronounce Mary. It wasn't her fault, so I tolerated her short comings." She said in a pathetic voice. 'I'm not as fortunate as you, I don't have a brother to take care of me. If I don't find work, I'm gone have to go back home.'"

"Pearl heard they were hiring at this new place called Elite Dining. It was a new restaurant that opened in an upscale hotel, called the Elite. Now, this place catered to White businessmen and officers. The manager, Cyrus K. Roux was from New Orleans, and was well known in the restaurant business for his success in managing five-star restaurants. I can't swear to this in a court of law, but he told me he was a woman, trapped in a man's body. You know what I'm saying?" Mary Alice said looking at Reba, with her head tilted, pursed lips and raised eyebrows.

Reba laughed and replied, "He was gay?"

"As a Jay bird, he spoke in a very soft voice; he was about 5'8" and heavy set, with thick, wavy black hair; his face was oily enough to fry chicken. He moved his hands and posed when he talked, as if he were an artist painting on a canvas. "But the one good thing about K (that's what he liked to be called) was that he was a civil rights advocate. He, in his infinite wisdom, decided he was gone hire a Negro to fill the Hostess position. In those days, we was only hired to work in the kitchen. But K thought it was his contribution to making a difference. He told me, 'since the Negroes are good enough to fight in the White man's war, then it's just the right thing to do.'"

"I met Pearl at the bus stop the next day she wore a freshly pressed white, short sleeved, front button blouse tucked inside a flared black skirt, she tacked a red strip of ribbon around the waist of the skirt (my suggestion) to accentuate her tiny waist, and she had a white scarf that was folded like a headband and tied around her puffy, pinned back hair, flat shoes, no hoses, and she always wore a pearl necklace."

"When she saw me, she said, 'Dang Mair Alice you always wearing a suit, you lookin like you goin to get a job as the boss.'"

"I laughed and told her, 'only if the money is right.' But she was tellin the truth, cuz I didn't go nowhere if I wasn't sharp as a tack, because I was the dressmaker's daughter. I had my hair pinned up in a French roll with soft curls around the front of my face and I placed the matching snood over the top of my head and behind my ears.

"What's a snood?" Reba asked.

"It was like a headband, my mom made it, she covered the

caps, used to make wedding veils, with the fabric to match my suit and it fit like a headpiece."

"Well my snood matched a charcoal gray gabardine suit that my mom tailor made to fit me to a T. The jacket had a center front closure with 5 pearl buttons, a curved yoke, nipped at the waist, with a pleated peplum, padded shoulders and cuffed sleeves. My finishing touches was a white no collar blouse, pearl earrings, with matching necklace and bracelet, hoses and a pair of black Mary Jane wingtips."

"Pearl, me, and four other Negro ladies got to the restaurant about 8:00 a.m. By the time 9 o'clock rolled around, there were so many people in that room I could hardly breathe, so I stood by the door. When K came out to choose people from the crowd, he pointed at me and said 'you the tall one in the suit by the door.' I pointed to myself, and he shook his head and pointed for me to go into his office. I looked for Pearl in the room and our eyes locked, and her little sleepy eyes were bucked as wide as she could open them and staring dead at me, like I stole somethin. I went into the office and K asked me, 'Darlin, can you read and write?' and I said, 'Yes.' He then told me about the hostess position that he wanted me to work, and I accepted because it was an opportunity I couldn't refuse, then I asked him, 'could you please hire my friend, she'll be a good worker and she really need a job.' K smiled and said, 'see I knew there was something about you Miss Mary, you got guts! K went out into the crowd and said, 'you with the red waistband, I like yoh style, come on back here and let me talk to you.'"

"Pearl and I usually went to work together, she was truly grateful to get that job in the kitchen, and wore that dreadful gloomy gray uniform with pride; and I never once mentioned that I asked K to hire her. I got dressed at work because my uniform was not something I would wear in the streets. Since I was a hostess, K said, 'I want my hostesses to wear something in vogue that screams, bon appétit!'" Mary Alice laughed as she tried to imitate his overly emphasized movements. "K was contrary, inside and out, he went right on about his business, as if he didn't care that there was a war ration on material, and had six peasant blouses, two for each of the 3 hostesses, made and shipped from New Orleans. They were white cotton peasant style blouses with elastic in the neck, with the big bell sleeves, and lace ruffles down the front and on the cuffs; three long black straight skirts; and three large black belts. He had us wear the blouse on the shoulders during lunch and off the shoulders during dinner and we had to wear 2" heels and he taught us how to walk." She burst into laughter. "He could walk in his heels better than any woman."

"Every payday I sent my dad money and cigarettes that I got free from the man that stocked the 'smooth smoking' machine. I figured that was far more than he was expecting, and if I sent him a steady flow of money, he would be partial towards me staying. You see my intension was to wait 'til the week before it was time for me to return home, and I was gone ask him, if he thought it would be better if I stayed in Cincinnati to work a while longer, so as I can continue to help out, because I can't find a job making this much money back home. My Bruh Shaw thought it was a good plan, and he said he would put in a good word for me by telling mom that he got mighty lonesome without family, and if it would be ok if I stayed a lil longer."

"I desperately wanted my parents' blessings, because whether they approved or not I had no intensions of ever returning to Pittsview; that is, other than to visit. I loved living in the city, and if I never saw another snake, agitated bull, intimidating rooster, or headless chicken running down a dirt road, then that would've suited me just fine. I enjoyed getting up each morning and having a job to go to, and making my own money. Even though I appreciated the time spent working with my mom, it was my time to experience being a single independent woman. I wanted to meet people, and have conversations, and experience something other than dressmaking, and caring for my sisters and brothers. And being under Bruh Shaw's watchful eye, and guidance was like putting icing on a cake—it only made it better."

"I enjoyed talking to the customers who traveled from one city to the other conducting their business. In the beginning, I envied how they got to travel and see the world, but the more I talked to them, the more I realized that traveling wasn't all it was built up to be. The ones that traveled regularly, seemed to be the loneliest, they would practically hold you hostage with their chatter about nothing in particular," She said in a sorrowful voice, "I stopped asking, them how they were doing, because some would actually tell me and in great detail." She said, with pursed lips and raised eyebrows. "The poor souls just repeated what their wives told them about their children, because they were never home to witness their child say his first word, take his first step, or attend any school activities. The regular customers and I watched their children grow-up through photographs, seemed like I knew just as much as they did about their own children. I can truly say, after a while, I didn't envy them at all. Hmm, I suppose that's why they say the grass always looks greener on the other side." She said while staring retrospectively into her past.

"I remember this one white man, who told me I looked like his daughter. I figured he hadn't been home in a while," Mary Alice began laughing, at her own joke, till tears ran down her cheeks. "He came into the restaurant and was seated in my section. I greeted him with my usual smile, and I said, 'Good day sir, I'm Mary Alice and I'll be your hostess for today.' He looked up and froze at the sight of me, his mouth was open but his words were stuck on the tip of his tongue. He stared at me and I stared back at him and I said, 'the soup of the day is chicken noodle, would you like something to drink?'

"He finally found his voice and replied, 'Hello, I'm well, thanks for asking,' he glanced at my name tag then said, 'Mary Alice.' So I asked him again, if he would like something to drink and I gave him his menu, then as I'm leaving he asks, 'Are you from Alabama?' and I replied briskly, 'No, sir' and walk away. I said no before I even heard the question, because I was thinking, what that got to do with me waiting on you?

"I didn't know, exactly, what was his problem, but I

reckoned it had to be an issue with a Negro, from Alabama, serving him. That is, in a fine respectable establishment as this one. At any rate, I asked a white hostess, Susan, to finish servicing his table because I didn't think he wanted me serving him. I continued working my other tables, talking and laughing with the customers, but the entire time I could feel the strange white man watching my every move.

"After about a half-hour or so, Susan came over to my station and said, as she pointed at the strange man, 'that gentleman would like you to come to his table.' Halfheartedly, I walked over to his table struttin like I was too blessed to be fooling with his mess, and I said, 'I hope you enjoyed your meal sir, is there anything else I can get for you?'

"A troubled and tired man looked up at me and said, 'No, I'm fine Mary Alice. However, I am curious as to why you gave your table to someone else.'

"Well, frankly sir, it was the expression on your face when you looked at me. I didn't think you wanted me to wait on you.

"Well that's just not true. Actually, I was shocked by the uncanny resemblance between you and my daughter.

"I was completely taken aback, by what he had said; but he either read the expression on my face, or my mind, because I was frowning, and I was thinking *'your daughter must look just like your wife, Mr. Blond hair, blue eyed, lily white man.'*" He started flinging his hands and shaking his head, like he wanted me to erase that thought, and he says, 'I know that sounded unbelievable, please allow me to explain. I have a seventeen year old daughter, and as I've watched you move about, even your mannerisms remind me of my daughter. My wife died a few years ago and it's been just my daughter, Raquel, and I. This year she graduated from high school and is attending the University of Chicago. I spoke to her today, and she informed me that after she graduates from college she wants to move to Europe, because she wants to see and experience the world before getting married and having children, and then she says, 'don't worry dad because I will not do anything that could possibly land me back in Omaha.' I don't know why I'm telling you all of this, when what I really would like to say is, I'm sorry.'

"I felt such sorrow for what I was thinking about this pathetic, delusional man that I told him, 'Sir your apology is accepted. I'm sorry for your loss; and please forgive me for misjudging you; and your daughter sounds absolutely lovely. Funny thing, your daughter and I are the same age and I know how she feels, I feel the same way about going back to my home town, Pittsview, Alabama.' At this point I figure we were sort of friendly, so I ask him. 'Do you have a photograph of your daughter, Raquel?'

"He turned as red as an apple, he jumped up from the table, grabbed his coat and brief case and said nervously, 'I'm sorry, I'm late. It was great talking with you.' He picked up his check and rushed to the register.

"I was dumbfounded and thinking to myself, 'he ran out of here like he saw a ghost. Lamb of God! White people know they're crazy.' At the time, I figured he was just troubled, so I said a silent prayer for the Lord to look over the strange man and his daughter.

"Before I could say Amen, I heard K calling me, 'Mary Alice, here you go' as he extended an envelope toward me, 'that man who was just sitting over there,' as he pointed to the table that Raquel's father, Dr. Jeckel and Mr. Hide was sitting, 'left you this envelope.' I opened that envelope and peeked inside and counted five one hundred dollar bills! I called upon my best poker face, took a deep breath and I folded the envelope and put it in my pocket. I thought to myself, *'thank you Jesus that I'm not white, because I would be as red as Raquel's father – Mr. What's-his-name.'* I didn't tell a soul that my rich uncle had gotten out of the poor house."

"So, who was he?" Reba asked, perplexed by the whole story of her mother looking like this white man's daughter."

"Child be patient, I'll get to that, all in due time. But right now, I think I needs to rest for a while. What time is it?

Bernice should be here soon."

5: BURY AND MARRY

It's a new day and time for Mary Alice's daily memory therapy session. Reba picked up where they left off the previous day.

"So mother, how long did you work in Cincinnati before you moved to East Chicago?"

"IT WAS JUNE 27, 1944 when I got the news. I'd been living in Cincinnati for about 2 years." Mary Alice said, as she blinked back the welled up tears in her eyes. It was a Tuesday, my day off, and I was resting in bed reading the last letter I would receive from my mother. In the letter, she wrote 'there are some things I want you to know before I leave this earth.' I was startled by a pounding, on the front door, so loud it could have awaken the dead.

"I jumped out of bed and screamed in the direction of the door, 'Just a minute, I'm comin.' I quickly put on my housecoat and house shoes. I nearly broke my neck running down the hall to the door. All the while, I'm thinking, the house must be on fire, or we were being attacked on the homeland. I opened the door and my eyes met a soldier standing at attention. The black band on his left jacket sleeve identified him as the grim reaper's postman. As I think back, I feel compassion for the poor thing. Not only for being assigned the task of delivering bad news, but more so for the nickname we had given him—Heartache."

"'Morning Ma'am,' he said looking through me."

"Good morning, Heartache." I replied, as I reached for the telegram he was offering me.

"He saluted me, turned an about face, and walked away. I closed the door and opened the telegram addressed to my brother."

"The telegram informed him that he had been granted a bereavement leave of absence. I got dressed, and went to the corner phone booth, and called the church back home. Miss Pearlie, the Mount Olive Baptist Church secretary, lead soloist, and usher answered."

"Hello, Miss Pearlie. How are you Ma'am? I waited, I knew bad news was quick to follow."

"'I'm fine, Baby. It's yoh momma.' She said, then screamed into the phone so loud, I had to move the receiver from my ear, 'Awe, Lord Jesus! What I'm gone do without my best friend?'"

"Then in a crying, while talking, voice she said, 'She took sick, sudden like on Sunday, and the Lord took her home on Monday. We waitin on you and Willie so we can commit her to her final restin place.' Miss Pearlie dropped the phone, and I could hear her screamin and just carrying on somethin terrible." Mary Alice was laughing as she reminisced.

"All the while, I'm shouting, 'Hello. Miss Pearlie,' while steadily having to put more coins in the phone. Now, I could only imagine what was going on with her. But, based on her past behavior during church services, Miss Pearlie was possibly sprawled over that floor, slain in the spirit. Mom use to get after Willie, for imitating her. But she was funny to watch. She was as wide as she was tall, one minute she would be directing the choir, then next she would take a dive and start rolling up and down the aisle."

"I can't remember how much money I feed that phone, before Pastor heard the commotion. Now, Pastor was 99 ½, if he wasn't 100, and was most too old to be trying to get her up off that floor, so he threw a sheet over her, like the ushers did when a woman was laid out under the power of the Holy Ghost. He finally picked up the phone, and I was able to leave my message, 'Please tell my dad, we will be home directly, and he can make funeral arrangements for this upcoming weekend.'

"Then Pastor prayed for traveling mercy; that the angels of the lord encamp around those that fear him; The Lord's Prayer, The Lord is my Shepard, he was still going when I ran out of coins. And Miss Pearlie was still carrying on through it all.

"Needless to say, but your Grandma Pearlie was quite vocal," she said to her daughter.

"That's just disrespectful, Ma." Reba said while laughing till her side ached."

"I went home, and got back in the bed. I thanked God for having my mom on this earth, as long as we did. Given how sickly she was, it was truly a blessing, and to have given birth to eleven healthy children. I pulled the covers over my head, and had myself a good ole farewell cry.

"Later on that day, I went to the restaurant and told K that I would be leaving for the funeral.

"He said, 'Sorry for your loss Mary Alice, take as much time as you need, your job will be waiting for you.' He held my hand and placed some folded dollar bills in my hand. I didn't look at it, but I thanked him and casually put it in my skirt pocket. Soon as I left the restaurant, I pulled it out of my pocket and counted 2-$100 bills! I immediately said, "thank you Jesus! You show been good to me.

"That evening, when Willie got home, I showed him the telegram. He hugged me and said, 'to be absent from the body, is to be present with the lord. I sure am glad we went home to see her one last time. Now, our only problem is getting home as soon as possible. The bus gone take a least four days.'

"I handed Willie a train ticket, that I bought for him with the money K had given me. Bruh Shaw gave me the strangest look, and said, 'Sis, where you get money from to buy train tickets?'

"I told him, 'K gave it to me.'

"'Sis, you know you got favor!' he said, hugging me tightly.

"That night, we boarded the train and went home to bury our mom.

"My mom had been sickly all her days, anyone who really knew

32

her was not surprise to hear that she had died. After she gave birth to my bruh Joe, her 8th child, her ailments turned for the worse. I know now, that she presented all the symptoms associated with high blood pressure, diabetes, and high cholesterol. Mix that together with carrying child after child, and you bound to have a heart attack, or the highfalutin name my doctor gave it—acute myocardial infarction.

"In those days, Negroes didn't have medicine available like we do now. My mom told me, 'when I was a child, Jack's grandma, Miss Louisa, was our apothecary, she had no formal schooling.' They say she had a gift, a God given ingrained ability, to mix concoctions that cured whatever your ailment."

"Really?" Reba said, in a bewildered tone as she wondered why no one ever thought to share this pertinent information."

A childhood memory of her dad emerged, of him combining clear whiskey, some other pungent smelling liquids, and rock candy cubes, which he let her drop into a large glass container, and he said to her, "this here, is what my grandma made me take, when I was a boy. It's gone kill anything that tries to attack you." Then he sealed the top of the container and put it in the window for a few days to let it 'mis-ke-o,' he said. After a few days, if one of us sneezed he would make us all take a spoonful. Reba smiled, because she recalled telling her daddy, 'Ronnie said, you gone kill us all with your concoctions.' She grabbed her iPad and asked Siri, 'define misceo.'

"Siri replied, 'misceo was a Latin derivative of the English word mix or blend.'"

"Thank you Siri."

"Reba, your satisfaction is all the thanks I need."

Reba raised her head, and straightened her posture, as a sense of pride inflated her self-image. Mary Alice watched, flabbergasted, as her daughter conversed with a computer.

"I was aware of my mother's condition because I spent the majority of my childhood, afterschool helping my mom with the dressmaking business, caring for her when her symptoms flared up, and I made sure my brothers and sisters were cared for, so as to not agitate my mom.

"I witnessed my mother's health rapidly deteriorate after the birth of my baby sister, Dorothy. Mom struggled through headaches, dizziness, shortness of breath, and excessive nose bleeds. She was completely bedridden while carrying Dorothy.

"Out of shear necessity, at the age of 12, I had developed into an excellent dressmaker, nurse, and homemaker solely because I wanted my mom to focus on getting better, and she did for a while. But when my brother and I went home for a visit, a few months before her passin, I could tell just by looking at her, that it was just a matter of time. I volunteered to stay home and care for her, but she firmly said, 'Mary Alice, you are a good daughter, and I appreciate all that you have done for me, and the children. But before I leave this earth, I want to see you have a better life, and that can't happen unless you leave the south. You are naturally smarter than most folks, cuz you got common sense, and that caint be taught in no book. And yoh wisdom is beyond your years. Conditions are slowly, but surely, changing for the better for colored people, so you needs to start thinkin bout yoh future. I want you to return to Cincinnati and I will talk to yoh daddy.'

"I felt guilty, for being happy because my mom thought she had to force me to leave. I didn't say a word, for a long while. Because if I did, it would have been 'yes' or 'ok,' anything contrary would've been a lie.

"Finally, my mom said, 'Mary Alice Upshaw, do you hear me talking to you?'

"And I said, 'Yes mom, I hear you.'"

"Bruh Shaw and I arrived in Alabama the Thursday before the funeral. My poor brothers and sisters were ill prepared to handle our mom's death. I understood why the younger ones were distraught, but Linda and Cora were acting as though they never knew she was sick. I had to take them to the side, and remind them of their responsibilities as the older children. And I know mom talked to them, because I was there. Then there was Miss Pearlie, she was just unmanageable, and not helping the situation at all. I told Jack and Son, 'Yall need to do somethin about yoh momma.' They laughed because they knew, that I knew, nobody could do a thang with Miss Pearlie, but get cursed out. Then there was my dad, he was just sitting there, stock-still, looking like he lost his best friend."

"So I started checking on the arrangements, and read over the obituary and it read: Willie B Upshaw was called home to glory on June 27, 1944. She leaves to mourn her husband Ervin Upshaw and 12 children: Willie Ervin, Ervin Jr, Linda, Mary Alice, Cora, Obie, Anna, Joseph, Daniel, Walter, and Dorothy."

"At the funeral, I mentioned to Miss Pearlie, (Mount Olive Baptist church's secretary, usher, and lead soloist) that the obituary was not correct. I told her, 'this should read 11 children.'"

"Miss Pearlie looked at me, as if she was contemplating taking her shoe off and hitting me in the head with it, for she was known to have a temper and didn't tolerate young folk disputing their elders. But I suppose, she had mercy on me during my time of bereavement, or she remembered where she was, and gently stated, 'Well baby it's too late to change it now, besides all dem children she had, an extra one wont hardly make no difference.' Miss Pearlie bucked her eyes and cocked her head; and I knew, from years of knowing yoh daddy's mother, that this was my sign to go sit down, conversation over. Miss Pearlie removed her usher gloves, and grabbed her choir robe as she wobbled to the front of the church, and sang, like an angel from heaven, Precious Lord. Everyone spoke very kindly about my mom and I remember someone read a really nice poem.

"The next day, or so Willie left for Cincinnati without me. I needed to stay, for a lil while longer, and get my family back on track. That evening, I went to the frog pond, and it was as if someone had pressed the pause button, on a universal remote control of their lives. I couldn't believe my eyes, the same group of Pittsview men, which were in the very same spot two years ago, were still talking about going up north. They had no new business, still drinkin' moonshine, and talkin' about how there was plenty of jobs up north for colored people. I listened as they hemmed and hawed, back and forth, with their liquor laced notions of how they, all twelve of them, were going to trail each other, 820 plus miles, mind you, up a road paved with prejudice and segregation." Mary Alice, Laughed while shaking her head.

"I didn't say a word, but I show was thinking, 'Please, y'all not gone make it to the county line, before Johnny Law stop all you Negroes for driving while colored.' You see, that type of foolishness, was a perfect example of the very thing I despised, about the boys in my town." She said, sincerely.

"And Jack, yoh daddy, was right there amongst them. He was a good man, but his one downfall, was following up behind his older brother. If Son wasn't hunting or drinking with his buddies, then he was fighting them or cheating with their girlfriends. He was always up to some devilment. However, I must say this, he tried his best to keep Jack away from his mischief. He would try to sneak away, threaten to kick his behind, but Jack was always right there, in the midst of it all.

"Yoh daddy, who they sometimes called 'Moon', was very handsome. In his youth he had light cocoa brown skin, fine curly hair, big brown eyes, and a long chiseled nose which he undeniably inherited from his grandmother, Louisa. He was a couple of inches taller than me, thin, but had brawny arms and large hands and the skinniest legs I'd ever seen." She smiled and paused, as if buffering her childhood memories from a preserved area of her brain.

"When I was growing up, I didn't have the time, nor the inclination to be fooling around with no boys. I had plenty of things to do to occupy my time, plus I thought the boys in Pittsview were just down right complacent, and void of a desire to move from that dirt road. If it were not for yoh daddy, constantly trying to get my attention and making me laugh," Mary Alice, chuckled, "I would have been bored to death with that bunch of pitiful Pittsview pickings.

"I remember as a young girl, I would take my brothers down

to the field to watch Jack and Son play baseball. Those two brothers knew they could entertain you with their clowning, and talking mess about the opposing teams. I must admit, they played as good as any major league baseball players."

"During this time, Jack was definitely sweet on me, and I on him. However, I refused to court him. I told him, 'I can't court you because you lack ambition, and you are perfectly content with living in Pittsview all the days of life.'"

"After we got married, it seemed like he repeated that story practically every day. Until I told him, if he didn't stop, I was gone leave him," she said jokingly. "He said, 'I didn't know what to say, so I didn't say nothing. But, I thought to myself, *I don't know what ambition means, and where the hell you think I should live?*' He just stared with his big brown eyes dumbfounded like a deer caught in the headlights. Then suddenly he leaned toward me and kissed me on my lips, and ran off like a young buck escaping a near death experience."

"I was pleasantly shocked and I yelled, 'You betta run,' as I walked home with a smile in my soul."

"He said, 'from that day forward, I considered you my girl since there wasn't no gang of Upshaw boys trying to kill me for kissing their sister.' And from that time forward we walked together to softball games, church, and other social events."

"Two weeks after my mother's funeral, I began thinking about returning to Cincinnati. But, my brothers and sisters were still adjusting to life without mom. They feared going into the bedroom where mom exhaled her last breath. When I was in her room, I saw a letter on her dresser addressed to me. It detailed her last wishes for me to take care of concerning the children."

"I gathered them all together in front of the double doors of mom's bedroom and said, 'it's time to let mom rest in peace.' I opened the doors, and her lonesome, dark oak, Victorian, queen size headboard was perfectly dressed in a white satin patchwork quilt with blue, hand-stitched inscriptions. The quilt was made from swatches of fabric from all the wedding dresses she made over the years. The first inscription, *Ervin & Willie Bee Upshaw* with *(October 9, 1920)* inscribed underneath, was centered at the head of the bed; then she grouped the children's names three in a row with our birthday underneath. Except the row with my name, a noticeable space was between my name and Cora, but it was not important at the time. I remember every one of their birthdays," as she began reciting. " *Willie Ervin (July 27, 1921), Ervin Jr (May 13, 1922)*, and *Linda (February 1, 1923)*; third row: *Mary Alice (July 8, 1925), Cora (Sept 18, 1927)*, fourth row *Anna (Nov 30, 1930)*, Daniel *(August 12, 1932)*, Obie*(Sept 23, 1933)*, fifth row: *Joseph (June 30, 1934), Walter (Oct. 25, 1936)* and Dorothy *(March 12, 1941)*."

"The children gathered around the bed, I sat Dorothy on the bed since she was only 3yrs old and not really aware of what was going on. I walked toward the dresser, which was located on the opposite side of the room, near a window draped in white lace curtains, and picked up an envelope that was labeled Willie B. Upshaw children. I told the children, 'this is a letter written by momma, she told me to read for our ears only.'"

"It said, 'Mary Alice is reading this letter to you, because I've gone home to be with the Lord. I want you to know that I love each and every one of you. I know you will miss me, but I don't want that to stop you from doing all you can do to make it in this world. I know you can make it because you have each other. I want yall to always remember, as long as you stay together, and help one another, I will be watching over you. Now Dorothy, my lil baby, it brings me much sorrow that I couldn't spend a few more years with her, so kiss and hug her for me every day and treat her extra special, for she's the one who will not remember me. And as she grows and start asking questions, I expect you all to answer them, truthfully. Yes, she needs to know the good and the bad. Now, I want you to stay in this room as long as you want today, but tomorrow is a new day, and all these things of mine will be put away for keepsake. Farewell my precious children, and remember, as long as you continue to believe in Jesus Christ, our lord and savior, I'll see you again, so be good. Love always, your mother." Mary Alice wiped away a tear that rolled down her cheek.

Reba was crying crocodile tears for the sorrow she felt for her uncles and aunts losing their mother during their youth; and tears of joy for having a strong mother in her life.

"The children slept in the room that night, and talked about all the good times with mom. How she would make them laugh, cry, and do the right thing. Dorothy laughed as she was jumping on the bed, as if she were on a trampoline, until she tired herself out, and fell asleep on top of mom's beautiful quilt.

"After that night, the children started doing better, and I started working on another plan, to get out of the south. I had a couple of options, I could go back to Cincinnati, or I could go to Chicago. My season for Cincinnati had come to an end. I was just about twenty years old and I was ready to be married. So I chose your daddy to be my husband, he just didn't know it yet.

"But, first I had to adjust some things in his life to make him the right man for me. The only thing keeping him in the south was his brother. His grandma Louisa, raised him, and she had died the year before, and he wasn't a momma's boy. So, the first adjustment was to move his brother out of Pittsview, then Jack would be more pliable to the idea of moving up north. I went down to the frog pond again to put a bug in Son's ear. "I asked him, 'what happen to yoh sis, Sang?'"

"'She still up in Detroit,' he says.'"

"'She doin alright? I mean, she aint havin no trouble with men messin with her pretty self, being that she out there all alone. You the last person I was expecting to see, when I got back home. I just knew you would be in Detroit, meetin all kinds of women, while you watching over yoh sis. Guess I figured wrong. Nice talkin to yoh Son.' Then I just walked away, and started talkin to my cousins."

"Son left for Detroit the next week. Jack and I started spending more time together talking about our future together."

"It was a few days before Christmas, Jack stopped by the house to take me for a ride in his new (to him) car. I wore a white ruffled blouse, red flare skirt, and black dolly shoes. As we were riding Jack said, 'Mary Alice, I bought this car with some of the money I've saved from fixing cars, tractors, and machines. I know you don't want to live in the south, and that you want a man that wants something out of life. Well I've saved up some money, I got three month's rent paid on an apartment, and I'm going up North. If you go with me, I promise, I'll never leave you, and I'll be the hardest working man you will ever meet.' I was busy listening and looking at Jack. It wasn't until he put the car in park, that I realized, we were in front of the court house.

"On December 21, 1944, we were pronounced man and wife. Three days later, at 3:00 a.m., we headed east on Glenville Road, turned north on highway 421, traveled 822 miles in 13 hours. We spent our first Christmas together in our one bedroom apartment in East Chicago, IN."

6: GROWN FOLKS BUSINESS

MARY ALICE MENTIONING SOMEONE had read a poem at her mom's funeral, jogged a childhood memory Reba had suppressed. It occurred during her last trip to visit her grandfather and his new wife, Miss Jane. She had kept this secret since she was 9yrs old, and had not revisited it since.

"Ma, do you remember when daddy, Aunt Sang, Ronnie and I went down south during our summer vacation?"

She scrunched her eyes and paused for a moment, while her brain was in search mode looking through 87 years of memories. Upon locating the segment of her life, that had transpired over forty years ago, her fascial expression relaxed.

"Yeees, that was the summer of 1968, the year Dr. Martin Luther, the King, that's what we called him, was killed. Jack loaded the car for his annual summer vacation. He only took you and Ronnie south that time. Course, he wanted to take the twins, but I enrolled those boys in summer school, bible school, and tutoring, because they clowned around, and got poor remarks on their Kindergarten report cards."

Reba smiled, as she witnessed her mom achieve this, once thought, simple task. She thought of how miraculous God had made mankind; and how most people take for granted, the processing involved in memory retrieval. But, she was humbled, after witnessing the effects of a stroke on her mom's brain, and the interrelated body functions.

"Ronnie and I hated going to the country and we begged not to go, but you said, 'You don't have a choice, get in the car. And make sure you say 'yes sir or no sir, when addressing my dad. And respect his new wife, Miss Jane.'" Reba said, imitating her mom.

"Yes, and you always thought you had the right to say whatever was on your mind. You asked me, while looking at the twins, 'Maw, if I was dumb, I wouldn't get to go, huh?' She said, imitating her daughter. "I was gone smack your face, if yoh daddy hadn't told you to get in that car. And, all the while, he laughin' at you. That is, until I had gave him the church usher eye, I wanted to smack him up side his head, too.

"As y'all was backing out the yard, the twins started crying, and waving goodbye. I told them boys, 'If you didn't think everything was funny, and did your work, you'd be going to. So stop all that crying, and get in the house. You made yoh bed hard, now you gone have to sleep in it.'

Mary Alice chuckled, "Those boys, with identical dumbfounded expressions, asked in unison, 'we got to go to bed, Ma?' I just shook my head, and pointed up the stairs.

"Then, as their going up the stairs, I hear Dawn whisper, 'its yoh fault, fool.' Dwan was already mad, so he acted like that was the straw that broke the camel's back, and he put Dawn in a headlock while yelling, 'and this fool, gone kick yoh ass!' They were the fightinist children you ever didn't want to meet. I made them go get they own switch, and I tore their lil butts up, and made them go to bed."

Their conversation was interrupted by the sound of the doorbell. "Oh that should be your physical therapists, we'll talk later." Reba, said as she left the room to let him in.

Reba was thinking about how much she hated going down south in her youth. Not just because it was too hot, too boring, and too long of a ride.

It was an absolute nightmare consisting of completely dark nights; aggressive roosters acting like they were pit bulls in another life; headless chickens running around the yard —was I the only one who thought this was not normal; runaway bulls that wanted to bully you, because your momma packed you a red outfit; and snakes-the devil himself. I was a city girl! I just wanted to ride my brand new bicycle, and swim in my in-ground pool. Neither of which I had, but I was a dreamer.

Ronnie said she was going to sleep during the entire trip, and when she woke up it would be time to go home. Well, sleeping beauty must have taken a sedative, because she mastered sleeping everywhere we went. I suffered from insomnia, onset by a severe case of fear and nosiness.

I remember it, like it happened yesterday, and I still get the heebie-jeebies thinking about it. The first time, Ronnie and I were riding in the back seat of Miss. Jane's car. She and her two friends, Big Sis and Lil Sis, were sitting up front.

These two sisters were as dark as the night, and they were big women. I can only assume, the big and lil, referenced their age differences. On their heads, they wore rags tied in the front, like they belonged to a gang; and they both had a wondering eye, so I never knew if they were looking at me. I believed my grandpa, when I overheard him say, they were blind in one eye, and couldn't see out the other. In retrospect, I believe that car ride with Miss Jane, or as they called her, 'School Teacha' was a highlight in their otherwise hum-drum lives.

The fairest one of all, Ronnie, was fast asleep, stretched across the back seat like an embalmed Egyptian princess, and using my lap as her pillow. Their whispering only made me listen more intensely, as I pretended to be asleep, with my head dangling forward, and intermittent snoring.

The second time, Ronnie and I were in grandpa's general store. My dad and grandpa were sitting at the counter area, located towards the front of the store. Ronnie and I were about 15 feet away, sitting in the dining area, resting our heads on a bare table, and fast asleep—well Ronnie, anyway.

I recalled hearing the same story, but from two different perspectives. Miss Jane's version was a love story, but my grandpa's version was more like a horror story. But, I guess that's what is meant when they say, "it all depends on how you look at it."

As we're riding, Big Sis starts talking about how excited she was to help with the upcoming anniversary party, for my Grandpa, and School Teacha.

"School Teacha, tell Lil Sis the story of how y'all got together."

"Child you see Mr. Ervin's grandchildren back there, I can't tell that story with them in the car." She whispered.

"They sleep." She said, as she turned around to look in the back seat. "Awe, that older one, sure is pretty, she lookin like a lil princess back there. I'll keep an eye on dem, if they wake up I'll let you know." As she lit another cigarette with the one she was finishing.

Lil Sis, egged her on, saying, "Yeah, School Teacha, I wants to hear the love story!"

"Alright ladies, calm down. But make sure you keep an eye on those children. Well, I'm not ashamed to admit it, I always had a yearning for Mr. Ervin, but his eyes were for Willie Bee, only. Mr. Ervin never said anything to me, other than a gentlemanly greeting. As a matter of fact, nobody really paid me much attention at all. I heard people referring to me as 'plainer than plain, Jane. You ladies know how it feels. But, unlike you all, losing the popularity contest, worked to my advantage, because it allowed me plenty of time to fully concentrate on obtaining a college degree in Education. When the government came along to appoint school principals, I was selected to be over the Pittsview territory, for colored people. This gave me great power in the community, and made ole Miss plainer than plain Jane quite noticeable."

"Fortunately, for Mr. Ervin, I was still sweet on him, when Willie Bee died. I admired his devotion to her. However, seeing that she left him to care for eight young children, I knew, before too long, he would be in need of a wife. Now, given his situation, I figured the above average looking women would run in the opposite direction. But, as far as I was concerned, his 8 littlle flaws, put him in a perfect position for my purposes."

"Willie Bee's funeral was a full-house, home-going celebration. I read a beautiful poem to the family, it left everyone in tears. During the repast, I approached Mr. Ervin and gave him a Christian hug and kiss on the cheek. Upon release I somberly held his hand, as I stared into his empty eyes and I said, 'I would like to speak with you about the education of the children, and some work that would allow you to spend more time with the children.' Ervin cordially replied, 'Yes, and thank you for coming.' I realized he wasn't really listening to what I was saying. Ervin's mind and spirit was numb with grief and his body was on auto pilot, just going through the motions of what appeared normal, and replying with words that sounded acceptable."

"So I watched and I waited. It took six months, but my opportunity, finally, presented itself. It was a Thursday, December 21, 1944, when I heard his daughter, Mary Alice, got married and moved away."

"I visited him on that Sunday evening, it was Christmas Eve. I arrived at 4:30pm promptly, wearing a beautiful purple dress that I purchased from the Sears catalog, a straw hat, and white lace gloves. I carried all my pots and baskets down that road. Ervin was sitting there on the porch waiting and watching me, like a hawk, as I walked down the road."

"It was a peaceful Sunday evening, I was sittin on the porch watchin the chickens frolic about as their roaster swaggered around, with his chest all puffed up, ready and willing to take on any predators. I looked up and saw someone from afar, walkin down the road, looking like a lost gypsy. As she got closer, I could see it was School Teacha, and I say to myself, '*where you headed looking like a hot mess*,' then she turns toward the house! And I felt a stabbin in my stomach. Causes me to stand straight up. I reckon I was in shock, cuz, I was her destination."

"I didn't react to his body language that was communicating surprise and possible discontent. I was totally aware that I was approaching Mr. Ervin when he was most vulnerable, and if he had the opportunity to think about it I wouldn't be standing on his porch."

"If I had only known her intensions, I wouldn't of been

home. But, since I had no way out, I was polite. So I says, "Hello, Miss Jane, what brings you around these parts?"

"He just stood there, like he was frozen, while I'm standing at his door, with baskets and pots in both hands. So I says…."

"Man, I was in a daze. I wanted to run away from home. Then she said,.."

"Well, Mr. Ervin I can see you forgot that I was bringing you, and the children, dinner today, but I really didn't expect you to forget your manners."

"I sprung forward, and opened the door and relieved her of her load."

'That was the first time I had been in his house, I found it to be a very large and clean home. I walked through the foyer, down the hall, turned right to walk through the living room, I finally reached the kitchen. He placed my things on the kitchen table. I grabbed an apron, from the hook on the door that led into the pantry. However, the strangest thing was the absence of his children. So I ask,"

"Will the children be home soon, Mr. Ervin?"

"Fraid not, Miss Jane, they are over to my Sis Rose house for the evening."

"I was thrilled to have him all to myself, but I didn't want him to know. So I converted my zeal into regret. And I said…"

"Ervin Upshaw, I do declare, you have ruined all my plans of cooking dinner for your children."

"Man, I was trapped all by my lonesome, I didn't know what to say to this woman. So I says, "I humbly apologize, but I plum forgot, but I haven't had supper, perhaps you and I can have a meal together. I was thinkin,

"I nearly peed in my pants from excitement!" They all burst into loud laughter, and immediately, shushed each other, and whispered, "The children."

She waited for the sisters to check that we were still asleep and then continued, "I prepared the table while Mr. Ervin washed his hands. I covered that god-awful looking dining table with my crisp white cotton tablecloth. I adorned that table with fried chicken, collard greens, corn bread, yams, macaroni and cheese, fried corn, mashed potatoes and gravy, fried okra and fried green tomatoes."

Lil sis interrupts, and ask, "Who cooked all that food?"

"I cooked it!" School Teacha said, in an agitated voice.

"Hmm. Really?"

"Don't talk out, lil sis, it'll be a long walk home, by yourself." Big Sis said, as if she had been put out before. "And I beg yoh pardon for her, School Teacha."

"Man I'm tellin you, she pulled everything, but a rabbit, out of that bag.' She covered my beautiful table, I guess so as not to get nothing on it. Hey, did I ever tell you, that was the door...."

"To the big house where your great-great grandma was a slave," my daddy says finishing his sentence.

School Teacha got quiet and Big Sis got nervous and yelled at Lil Sis, "See what you done did, apologize!"

"I apologize, then what happened, School Teacha?" Lil Sis replied insincerely.

"Then, Mr. Ervin reached for my hand, as he prayed over the food, his mere touch caused my body temperature to rise. I thought my fight/flight system was malfunctioning. As we're eating, I looked over to him to say something, and I got all tongue-tied, so I just put my head down and continued eating. But then he says..."

"Anyhow, I noticed she was bashful. So, I starts some small talk, cuz that's what a gentleman does, cuz you gots to make a woman feel comfortable. You know what I'm sayin? So I says..."

"How is the new job coming along?"

'Hot damn! What I say that foe. I thought she was gone talk till the cows come home. I didn't think I was gone get anything else in that evening. You know what I'm sayin?' They both roared with laughter.

At the time, I didn't understand what was so funny. But in retrospect, I realize my grandpa thought he was a playah; and my daddy abetted in his dramatization, with his incorrigible laughter.

"I wasn't shy when it came to my job. Because, yes I am proud of my college education, and for being chosen for the position of school principle, in charge of all the Russell County colored school children. Yes, I am a colored woman in a position of power. I am in charge of all the funding and disbursements. Yes, I am privileged and some colored folk may even say wealthy."

Then for a long period of time there was silence, they were as quiet as church mice. I peaked, and the princess was still fast asleep. I snored again, just in case they were thinking I was awake. However, in retrospect, I can only deduce, while School Teacha was giving herself one accolade, after another; sounding and looking crazy, even to the sisters; she realized, albeit too late, that she had gone too far. She regained her composure, and tucked in her crazy. Then, proceeded as if it never happened.

"So anyways, I told Mr. Ervin, 'I'm enjoying my new position as school principle, in charge of all the Russell County colored school children. I'm enjoying the opportunity to learn more about how the school system is designed. I have plans to change the way our children are being taught. That was one of the things I wanted to talk to you about. The government has given our school district a grant, to pay for books and supplies, and a school bus, and we are in need of a bus driver. I thought of you, because it would give you an opportunity to have more time with your children, and the hours won't interfere with you running your general store."

"I was trying to read his reaction, but he never looked up from his plate."

"I heard what she was sayin, but I was thinkin it through. Cuz, I knew there had to be more to it, than what she was sayin. You know what I'm sayin?'

"So I said, 'I also wanted to tell you, I'm in a position where I hear lots of information, about ways to make more money, so that colored children don't have to continue to struggle, that is they can have some start-up money."

"Bingo! Now I looks up, cuz she was talkin my language. Cuz, I show didn't need no bus drivin job. I'm Big Ups, I don't get around like that. You know what I'm sayin?" They both roared with laughter.

I was concerned my daddy's loud laughter would awaken Ronnie, so I began squirming in my chair, and my dad quieted down.

In a shush voice, Grandpa continued, "I took a swig of her too sweet lemonade, to help me swallow her ok-tastin food, and I slowly wiped my mouth. Then, I looked up at her and I say, 'Please continue Miss Jane, I realize I'm not sayin much, but I am payin attention, it's just that yoh food is as good as yoh conversation is interesting.' And she says…"

"Thank you Mr. Ervin, save some room for dessert, I made peach cobbler and a chocolate cake."

Big Sis said, "Okie, dokie, smokie! Now we gettin to the good part—dessert. They all laugh and shush one another, and Big Sis whispers, "Go head tell it, School Teacha."

"You really needs to get you some, and stop all that secondhand living through School Teacha," said Lil Sis in a humorous (but I'm really serious) tone.

'So, I'm bought full now, and you know what a gentleman really wants for desert.'

They both get real quiet, so I figure they must be looking over at the table, to make sure we're asleep, so I give them a nice, big, reassuring snore.

So I says, "Miss Jane, I do declare, I haven't had a meal this good since Willie B passed on to glory. Then I looks real sad."

"No, you didn't play the widower card?" asked my daddy.

"Yes, I did." Grandpa said in a hushed voice, "It's gone expire after 9 months."

Grandpa began talking too fast, and my daddy was laughing too loud, for me to hear. I was already struggling to understand his southern twang, under normal conditions. So I began turning my head, like I might awaken from the noise.

For a moment, the room was instantly mute. Grandpa continued, but much quieter.

"She touched my leg and says…"

"Then, I noticed his mood changed like he was in mourning. So, I put my hand on his leg, out of compassion, it was a perfectly innocent gesture, and I asked him, "How you been holding up these days?"

"Then, sorrowfully and slothfully I say, 'I'm doin. Gets mighty lonesome tho, without a mate. I suspect, seein' I have all these children, I needs to remarry. And it's only natural, that a man has needs. I hope you don't mind me being so outspoken, but I feel comfortable talkin to you, Miss Jane.' I puts my hand on her hand, which was on my leg. And I says, 'I trust your opinion, cuz you an intelligent woman, and know more than all the folks around these parts.'"

Then my daddy says, 'You a smooth ole dog.'

I was tempted to get up and tell him, 'Hey, I got smacked for calling Twin a dog,' until I considered the penalty for eavesdropping on grown folks business. Besides, grandpa laughed at being called a dog.

"Girl, I'd swear before Jesus! His hand, on my hand, which was on his leg, brought out the boldness in me. And I said, 'Well, thank you Mr. Ervin, I feel honored that you feel so highly about me. I've always respected you, also. And, I'm a straight forward type of woman myself, which leads me to what I really want to discuss with you. I've had feelings for you, since I was a young girl, and I haven't felt that way about a man, since. So what I'm trying to say is, we are both lonely people that can help one another. If you know what I'm saying. Our eyes locked and I saddled Mr. Ervin and landed on top of…..."

At this point, I feared if I listened to anymore of their grown folks business, I would be scarred for life.

Since, I didn't have a frog to awaken the princess, I started coughing, (the choking on one's spit, while sleep coughing), in Ronnie's face. The princess awaken from her deep sleep, screaming like a wicked witch. Then I screamed, "Sorry!" as I covered my head, because I really needed to laugh, and I knew she was going to smack me. My arm hurt for a while, but it was worth it, to get those women to stop talking.

Big Sis and Lil Sis turned around, asking in a concerned tone, "you ok, baby?" But, their facial expressions were saying, "hit her for me, too."

"Yes sir, Ole School Teacha was a wild thang, don't let the plain Janes, fool yah. She wrestled me down, like a steer 'bout to be branded, and just took it. You know what I'm sayin?"

"After three months, of Sunday dinners, while the children visited Sis Rose. I found it best to make an honest woman out of her. My Willie Bee, wasn't comin back, and School Teacha made me an offer I couldn't refuse. She was teachin me the white folk's way, and I was payin attention. Besides, she was putting a few extra dollars in my pocket, on the regular. Yes sir, for what I was getting out the deal, I's be they first colored bus driver in the county, to drive all dem loud taz kids. You know what I'm sayin?"

"So, what she teach you?'"

"Well, I guess I needs to tell somebody," he said in a whisper. "But, Jack, this for yoh ears only. You know what I'm sayin? We has this plan called P.O.O.R. it stands for, Plan On Our Reparation. Miss Jane overheard some white folks talkin bout it. You know they think they can say anything around us, cuz they figure we either dumb, or stupid. You know what I'm sayin?"

"So, these white folks talkin bout progress. They say as time passes, things change and the lumber, and the land be sold, to build highways, houses, and such. This progress, will cause folks to have to move, but colored folks wont get nothing for their troubles, cuz we don't own no property or land."

"Somehow, she came upon, the surveyor's map that these white folks had while they was talkin. This here map, layed out all the sections of property around Pittsview that had been deeded. Miss Jane says, according to the layout on the map, they aint lookin at the land where colored folk livin, so the time was just right for P.O.O.R. to startup. She says, our land is full of lumber, our soil is rich and a highway through these parts would make the route much shorter to Georgia."

"Now, every other month, ever since we got married, if you know what I'm sayin, I goes to the surveyor's office and get a deed notarized and filed in our name. I was frightful the first time I went down there, but just like Miss Jane told me, they figured I was runnin the errands of the Boss-man."

"How much land y'all own?"

"Inside!" Somebody, yells from the outside.

"Hold on Jack, let me go out here and get this package."

"Daddy, how much longer we gotta be here? Daddy, this is too boring, I can't take much more of this God forsaken place." Ronnie said, in a whining voice, as she was awaken by the sound of the screen door, as it slammed shut, upon Grandpa's exit.

"That evening, my daddy took us to spend the remainder of our vacation with relatives in Columbus, Ga. They lived in a less rural environment with fenced backyards, sidewalks, and the children wore shoes."

7: ANTE INSANE

"MAW I REMEMBER WHEN Ante Sang would try to tell me about her younger years, but you always stopped her before she could finish. Why is that?"

"Because I didn't want you listening to crazy stories and then trying to go out and act like her."

"Yes, now that I'm a mother, I can understand your concern. That an impressionable child would try to reenact some of her ridiculous narratives. Personally, I always thought the tales were a bit on the bizarre side of crazy. I was traumatized after the first story when I was about 8 years old. She told me about an encounter with this woman who was known for cutting folks, and was itchin to slice her across her face.

"Well, Ante Sang said, laughing, as if she was about to share a hallmark precious moment, 'When I saw her coming my way, that's when I remembered, clear as day, that I left my knife in my other purse. You see, right before leaving I decided to change my shoes and of course I had to have the matching purse. Nah, I had to think fast. So, before she could finish her speech, so as to gather a crowd of spectators.

' I took off my left shoe, so as I would have balance when I reached back, and using the heel of my shoe, I started beatin the hell out of that wretch. I put a real whippin on her that night.'

"She looked into my eyes, and I stared back at my Ante's face that was heavy laden with regret. Then she spoke in a remorseful tone, 'Baby girl, I tell you the truth, I learned my lesson. And this is why I'm here this day to tell you,' she raised her hand, 'hand to Jesus, make sure you have a knife in every one of your purses.'

"Ever since that first episode, I've referred to her as Ant Insane. Try it, if you say it really fast you can't hear the difference. I was a sensitive child, I had no business hearing that kind of stuff. But I loved to see her coming, so I could hear another one of her tales. I guess she was my amusement park roller coaster. I'd stand in line, willing and waiting to be frightened, as she slowly guided me to the top of the hill. I'd close my eyes, while praying to Jesus that I didn't throw-up; and scream for my momma and daddy to save me. Because I knew I was about to be dropped into an abyss at the speed of light. Then the horror was finally over, and I would swear never, never again. Until the next time I saw her, inexplicably excited to be terrorized. I still think about that poor woman being beat with her shoe. I hope and pray, she made that story up."

"Pleeeze, you'd be better off hoping someone will ring the doorbell, and give you a million dollars in small bills. Child that story was true to a fault, and that poor woman had lil patches of hair missing, bout the size of Sang's heel, over the top of her head." Mary Alice laughed, "Patchess had to wear a wig ever since that night."

"Patchess? Her name was Patchess? Reba asked dumbfounded.

"Everybody in the neighborhood started calling her Patchess. I don't remember her real name." Mary Alice said as she paused with a query expression. "Nope, I got nothing. That's why I don't like nicknames. But, you don't know half of the stuff yoh Ante Sang been through."

"Thank God I'm stronger," Reba said, with a poker face as she placed her hand on her queasy stomach.

"I remember when Sang lived in Detroit, back in 1949. I remember the year because I was pregnant with your sister, Bay-Bay. It was the Saturday morning before Memorial Day, Jack was loading his 1942 Buick, Roadmaster for a trip to Detroit, Michigan, to see his sister, Sang. He took our two babies Jack, Jr. and Sarah Louise. They was about two and three years old. He was a proud father and wanted his sister to meet her niece and nephew. I wasn't joining him on this trip because I could use the break to rest. Plus, my bruh Daniel had just arrived at our house, two weeks prior, so he could start his new job at U.S. Gypsum. Jack's boss told him about the position while they were out fishing, Jack told me, and I called my Dad to see which of my brothers were ready to come up north. Daniel arrived the next week and started working that following Monday."

"As you well know, Jack was crazy about his sista and she was crazy about him. Sang called him every Sunday around 6 p.m., just like clockwork. He would laugh, as if he were being tickled, as Sang gave him the play-by-play details of her latest jaunt. She was cordial towards me, because even though we were from the same town, we never had any direct contact, other than when Sang dropped-off her dresses with my mom for alterations."

Back in the day, Sang was a sight to be seen. She had that light, pass for white, flawless skin – you know, like the color of a cup of cream with a teaspoon of coffee. Eyebrows that bowed toward her inner eye and slightly arched as it reached to the opposite end of her large almond shaped eyes. Her naturally dark red hair, glistened with golden highlights, perfectly streaked by Alabama sunshine. It was stylishly cut in 3"locks, and gracefully framed her face. Her nose was noticeably long, and unusually narrow -that is, for colored folks; and thin lips—that is, for colored folks. All of that may not have been so hard for the other women to take, if God had not flirtatiously placed a small black beauty mark on the right side of her top lip. Especially, since that was the only color on her that resembled the majority of the colored folks around our neck of the woods."

In addition to having 'the face of an angel,' as her daddy would say, Sang grew up to have the body of a harlot, 34-24-38, and all of the 38" rounded up in the circumference of her butt, and I declare it was as round as a basketball – but not so unusual for colored folks. And all of that rested on a pair of big shapely legs."

"She wore beautiful dresses made from the finest materials and she requested the same alterations made to every dress. At the time, I wondered where in world she was getting all these fine dresses. I would hear her tell Mom, 'Memaw, (that's what Sang called her) I got some more dresses for you to work yoh magic on.' Mom altered all her dresses, and she had way more than her fair share, along with coordinating lace slips that landed at the top of her calf. Mom created a style just for Sang, her own signature look, if you will, by accentuating her small waistline and allowing the lace around the bottom of her slip to peek from underneath her dress so as to bring attention to her very shapely legs. Her stylish ways prompted much gossiping amongst the decent good Christian folks at Mount Olivet Baptist Church. Those church ladies had a field day talking about her."

"One would say, 'It's just downright shameful for a lady to showcase her underwear.'"

"And then yet another Christian would say, 'It just aint right for a single woman to be hangin out with a bunch of men at BBB's, I suspect they gettin more than they haircut.'"

"But Moma told Sang, as she rhymed and snapped her gum, 'Baby, don't you give no mind to what those ole biddies got to say, [snap!].

Cuz it aint about what you wear, anyway. [Snap! snap!].

They can take yoh clothes, then they'll have to complain bout yoh lil waist, and yoh big hips [snap!].

Or yoh red hair and lil lips [snap!].

Irregardless of yoh peek-a-boo slip [snap! snap! snap!].

It really don't matter what you wear, cuz their no good-for-nothin' man, still gone stare [snap!].

Cuz yoh beauty is one of your gifts, I'm only adding a lil lift with this [wink & snap!] peek-a-boo slip [snap!].

Truth be told, they all just peas in pod, and they aint mad at you, they mad at God [snap! snap!, snap!].'

Sang and my Mom embraced, and burst into laughter."

"Sounds like Memaw was a rapper." Reba said, laughing as she raised her index finger to pause her mother's train of thought. "It seemed as though Ante Insane and Memaw were very close. Do you know why she called her Memaw? Where did she get all the clothes? And why was she hanging out at a barbershop?

Mary Alice appeared agitated by the questions. Reba made this assessment, based on the frown on her face and the mean mug starring back at her. Her suspicions were confirmed when her mom said, "Stop asking so many questions, and just listen. I'm gone get to that, you can't get nowhere fast puttin the cart before the horse."

"Alrighty then! There may be no such thing as a stupid question, but there's something to be said about untimely ones," Reba thought, as she chuckled, to herself."

"So, I was in the bedroom taking a nap and all of a sudden, I'm awaken by my Bruh Daniel shouting, to the top of his lungs."

"What are you talking about?" Reba thought, but didn't dare ask.

"'Mary Alice, telephone it's some lady, named Willie Louise!' Daniel screamed again, louder than before. I came into the room, and slapped him in the back of his head and said, 'boy what I tell you bout screamin, like you done lost yoh mind?' Daniel, looking all dumbfounded while rubbing his stinging head, cried, 'Dang Mary Alice I covered the ear piece, she didn't hear me.' I rolled my eyes at him as he quickly left the room. I took a deep breath, while saying a silent prayer for patience and for the safety of Jack and my babies. Because the devil was tryin to make me believe, that this call must be bad news. Sang only calls to talk to her baby brother, never directly to me, and Jack should have been there with her. I exhaled and said, 'Hello.'"

"Hey Mary, this Sang. I just called to say that you and Jack are doing a great job with these kids. They are the sweetest babies I've ever seen, I just love how Sarah calls lil Jack, brother, like that's his name." Sang thought that was the funniest thing. She said, "It reminds me of how my daddy started calling my bruh William, Son, and now everybody calls him Son. And as you know, my name is Willie Louise, but they tell me I got the nickname, Sang, because I started singing before I could walk.

Sang laughed joyously, "yep I loved to sing and daddy would say, 'Sang baby, sang!' and my nickname stuck like glue."

"Well thank you Sang, for saying that about the children, your brother manages them very well. And you're right how nicknames can stick to a person. I have some relatives that I don't even know what they're birth names are, because we've been calling them lil Sis, Tug, and God help us, there's one named Titty boy."

Mary Alice laughed and Sang hollered in unison.

"Nah that boy gone have as much trouble tryin to cut that name loose as he must of had lettin his moma's titty loose," Sang roared with laughter. "Well, I'm really glad Jack brought them along, I'm really enjoying them. Maybe next time you can come along with them."

"Yes, I will surely do that."

"Ok, hold on, Jack wants to holler at you. I'll talk to you soon, love you sis."

"'All right. And umm, love you too.' I said in a state of shock in response to her words of affection. But, I was feeling really good after that call. For one, Jack was a good father, and because Sang and I had become friends—or at least friendly."

After I hung up the phone, I was too excited to lay back down. I started baking some tea cakes as I revisited, in my mind, the call from Sang. I felt too good for my bruh Daniel to be hiding from me in his room. I knew the smell would remind him of mom, and no words of apology could be better suited. He came into the kitchen as soon as I took the first batch from the oven, sat down and helped himself to the platter of tea cakes that I placed next to a large glass of milk.

"So who was that lady, you was talkin' to on the phone, sis?" Daniel said while chewing with his mouth full.

"Jack sista Sang, you most too young to remember her." I replied, resisting the urge to scorn him for his poor manners.

"Oh my goodness, yes I do remember her," he said with a devilish smile on his face.

"Boy, when Sang left Pittsview, you was around ten years old. How you remember her?" I asked him, as my baby kicked me for luring his no mannered, lying behind out of his room.

"I's member her like it was yesterday," he replied, with lust in his eyes as he leaned his head back and closed his eyes, "I was sitting on the porch steps, playin my guitar, and I saw her comin up the way. I started strumming those strings, keepin in time with her hypnotizing hips, that she was swaying, special like, just for me. She was smiling at me as I played and stared at her. When she reached me, she leaned real close to my face, as she dragged her fingers from the top of my head down to my neck. And then she say "Hey handsome, is yoh moma home?"

"You could've poked me with a fork, cuz I was done and dumb. All I could do was shake my head up and down. I thank God, to this day, I didn't go blind, cuz as she went up the stairs, I got a close-up of her fine, big legs. She was the star in my dreams that night....OUCH!" Daniel shouted in reaction to the pain he felt from the slap that I landed upside the back of his head. "What you hit me for this time Mary Alice?"

"I got up in his face, and while looking him directly in his eyes, with the meanest look I could muster-up, I says, 'Boy! You teeterin on bein disrespectful you best go wash yoh mind, befoe I beat you behind.'"

"We both burst into laughter, because he knew I was acting like our mother. Those words were so familiar to him because my mom seemed to say that daily to my brothers and most often to him. You see, Daniel was very handsome and had a head full of thick curly hair that attracted the females of every age, and he loved the attention. We laughed until we cried in loving memory of our mother. I could feel her spirit fill the room, as if she was right there looking over us. Daniel said, 'Mary Alice for some reason talking about momma helps, cuz I've been missing her something awful.'"

"I told him, 'That's quite natural, Daniel, that's yoh momma, and yah only get one, and thank God for the time you got. We should never stop talking 'bout our memories of momma, it keeps her alive in our hearts. And allows us to release any sadness that could get bottled up inside you, and make you feel too tired to move.'"

"About a year later, Jack told me what really happened after he hung up the phone. But, by this time, Sang and I had really became good friends." Mary Alice chuckled, as she looked straight ahead, as if she were watching a rerun of her yesteryears. "When Bernice was born, Sang carried on something shameful at the hospital, because our baby looked like she had spit her out. I was going to name her Willie Louise, and Sang was already calling her lil Sang. But yoh daddy said, 'No, I want to name her Bernice.'"

'Uh, Jack who you know named Bernice?' Sang said angrily, as she stared at him, with a smirk on her face, eyes squinted, and hands fisted tight. If she had heat vision, like superman, she would have burnt him to a crisp." Mary Alice said, laughing at her own joke.

'I had a dream, and Grandma Louisa told me to name her Bernice. She says, when it's all said and done, I will understand why.'

Sang replied, "hmph," totally unimpressed by Grandma Louisa's re-appearance.

Reba opened her mouth to ask a question. But, upon recalling the unwelcomed response she had just received a moment ago, forbade her words from venturing beyond the tip of her tongue. However, her trusted intelligent assistant, Siri, was always willing and waiting to answer all her questions. Reba, spoke into her phone, as her mom observed with a look of annoyance.

'Siri, what's the meaning of the name, Bernice?' Reba felt her mom staring, but resisted looking at her.

"'Checking my sources,' Siri replied in a cheerful voice. 'Alright! I found this on the web for Bernice name meaning.'

Reba read the results aloud, "The French, American, biblical and Greek meanings are all the same—the one who brings victory."

"Thank you Siri." Reba said as she spoke into the phone.

'It is I, who should thank you,' Siri replied.

Reba smiled as she looked up into her mom's astonished facial expression.

'That's a smart phone,' Mary Alice said, as she smiled.

"Well, we thought that was it, and our baby girl was all set, as Siri said, to bring about the victory," Mary said as she chuckled, "until they gave me her birth certificate when I was leaving the hospital. Turns out Sang didn't think much about Grandma Louisa's opinion – alive or dead. After she cursed out Jack, we thought she stormed out of my hospital room and went back to Detroit. But, she first spoke with the head nurse. Passin' as a white woman, she told them that I was her maid, and she wanted to submit a name change."

"How could that be possible?" Reba asked.

"It wasn't uncommon back in those days. If white folks said it, then there was no questioning it."

"Jack was so mad at Sang, that he wanted me to be mad at her, too. He said, "you member when you talked to Sang that time when I took Sara and Brother to Detroit? Well, after I hung-up the phone, she says to me, 'Ok I talked to yoh lil sidity wife. Now, will you go out with me tonight?' She started imitating the way you answered the phone, 'Hello, I'm very proper, I can talk like a white woman.' She was laughing but I wasn't, and I told her, 'Sang stop talkin bout my kid's moma around them. Besides, don't act like you jealous of my wife cuz she smart, she just wants a better life for me and our children.

For a long while we just sat there on the couch, it was so quiet you could hear the clock ticking the minutes away. She knew I was upset, and she knew I wasn't gone talk to her until she made things right."

"'I started gathering the kids' stuff, and putting it in their bag, cuz I was gettin' the hell up out of there. Then she finally says, 'I'm sorry, I was just kiddin around, and sometimes I play too much. But I see you love your wife, and you not gone let nobody disrespect her. I promise it will never happen again. As I sat on the arm of the couch watching the children play with one another, it made me think of how much I have to be grateful for, and how important you are to me. My heart would be broken if I never saw or talked to you again. Her eyes welled up with tears, and her expression was mournful.'"

"'I felt such an awful heartache, because Grandma Louisa, and Memaw was gone forever. And moreover, cuz I was gone let my foolish pride let you walk out that door. But then, as I thought about the time I spent with them, the memories eased the pain. As if they weren't gone forever, because they came alive through my recollections. And through the children, I noticed how much they resembled you, with their narrow nose, and large eyes that undoubtedly trickled down from Grandma Louisa. And they got their creamy whipped, peanut butter smooth skin from Memaw. It's as if they were saying hello, through your children. That's why I caint never let us part angry, you is my baby brother and nothin', including my own nonsense, gone get in the way.'"

"'You know I aint got nothin' against Mary Alice, her mother was like a mother to me. She helped me when I was feeling dejected and rejected. I remember her chewing gum and snappin' and poppin' it, like there was no tomorrow as she gave her words of encouragement.

"'Baby there's a price to be paid for natural beauty, [snap!]. People are going to despise you for no reason, [snap!] other than that they want what you have [snap!]. It's a gift when you're dealing with men, [snap! snap!] and a curse, when you dealin' with women, [snap! snap!!]. So take the good with the bad, and use it to get what you want out of life [snap! snap! snap!].

"I remember my first haircut. I always wore my hair pulled back in a ponytail or bun, because I didn't know how to style it any other way. Everybody said I had pretty hair, but to me it was a curly heap of trouble. I was about eighteen when Memaw handed me a copy of a bridal magazine and said, 'see that lady's hair, it's time you make a change. I can see you with short hair. Your head and facial features are small, yep, you could wear your hair curly all over [Snap!]. All you'll need to do, to keep it up, is wet it and rub a dab of olive oil through yoh hair. Finger comb while styling the curls around your face with your fingers and you'll be set for the rest of the day, [Snap!].'

"'I thought it was a good idea and I didn't mind doing anything that would get the good Christians stirred up. And that very next Sunday, I intentionally arrived at church after the choir sang their A&B selection. I sashayed my way up to the third pew, with my new short hairdo, baby blue dress, red belt, and a red peek-a-boo lace slip. Out the corner of my eyes, I could see husbands being elbowed by their wives for gawking at me.' Sang burst into laughter.'"

"'Her total recall was cut short by a loud knock at the door. I wasn't surprised that it startled the children, but she didn't even look in the direction of the door. I mean she completely ignored it, as if she didn't hear it. So, after they knocks again, I say, "Are you gunna' get that? She smiled, hugged me and then put me in a head lock, like she did when we was kids, and said, 'say you forgive me and I'll let you go.' Naw, I forgave her without question, I didn't even question her regarding her ways, but I aint doin' it no more. She done crossed the line, Mary Alice.'" Jack was furious."

"Well, by that time, Sang and I had truly become friends. Besides, she had already shared what happened that day, and much more with me. Had she not, I suppose, Jack could have got me all flustered. That's why it's not wise to be so quick to judge people, and jump on their band wagon without considering all of the facts."

"Yoh daddy intentionally did not tell me everything that happened that night. Therefore, far as I'm concerned it's a lie by omission." Mary Alice chuckled. "First, he would've talked till I felt coarse towards his sista. Then, after they makeup, he'd be tellin' me how I shouldn't hold a grudge. I wasn't born yesterday, and aint nothin' new under the sun, especially when it comes to sibling rifts. I had too many sisters and brothers, not to be wise to his tomfooleries."

"He failed to tell me, Sang whispered, 'It's probably White Riley, or Cracker Craig.' As she lit a cigarette and blew rings of smoke to amuse the children, while ignoring the knocks. 'Yeah, they come by every Saturday. One to pay, and one to collect, but he ends up paying too. I have an account at the downtown furniture store, and they comes by to give me $25.99 for my couch and my baby grand piano that you see sittin' pretty in the living room.'"

"Then the man on the outside screamed, 'Sang open the damn door!'"

"Jack recognized the voice. Sang yells back at the voice, 'Just cuz you knockin, don't mean I have to let your asss in,' as she walked to the door and opened it."

"There stood Son looking like a mirror image of his father, Huddy. His freshly shaved face was the color of golden wheat, almond shaped, brown eyes, narrow long nose, thin lips and oversized hands. He wore a brown fedora hat, three piece brown single-breasted suit with wide notched lapels, baggy pants with cuffs, button-on suspenders, crisp white shirt and brown & white round toe shoes. Son was 5'9" but his athletic build combined with the large cigar that he secured with his front teeth made him appear taller.

"'Sang! What have I told you bout just opening a door without asking who it is?" yelled Son.

Sang laughed as she held the door opened with one hand and beckoned him to enter with the other.'"

"'Boy, I knew it was you. You knock like the building on fire, and you come over here the same time practically every day. Come on in here, and see your brotha and his kids.'"

"'Son did as she instructed, Jack and Son shook hands then embraced.'"

"You see, she knew Jack was dumbfounded at the sight of her, and where she lived. She figured he wanted to ask, but didn't have the nerve. Sang's lifestyle had changed when she decided to move to a town where nobody knew her. And she got a kick out of playin' too much, and Jack was a perfect target, because he saw everything as right or wrong, no in-betweens. It's difficult to explain her craze with being in control whether it be her bro or foe."

"Jack put the kids to bed that night at Cousin Ruth's house, because he and Son escorted Sang to her club, 'The Club.'"

"They arrived at The Club around 9:00 p.m., and the joint was packed! Fortunately, Sang had a reserved table, located at the front and center of the stage. The music was loud, and the people were louder and everybody was smoking and drinking alcohol. And rightfully so, cuz it was Saturday night, the one day of the week that colored people let their hair down, and forgot bout their troubles for a lil while."

"'I hope this heifer can sing, cuz I could be anteing in at the gambling joint.' Son said, as they made their way through the thicket of people jammed inside The Club. As they passed by this couple, Son shook the man's hand, and winked at his date. Sang saw her slip a matchbook into his breast pocket—a common style used by cheaters to pass messages."

"'Boy, please you aint slick,' as she rolled her eyes at Son. 'Jack this gal, right here, is hot as fire, and she can saaang her tail off!'"

"'She must be something else, cuz you don't give no praise when it comes to singing, unless they sho'nuff something,'" said Jack.

"'A half-naked waitress with child-bearing hips in fishnet stockings, and high heels, arrived at the table and said, 'Good evenin' folks! Can I get yall something to drink?'"

"'Yep-yep,'" said Son with a devious smile as he nudged Jack, "'I'll take you, straight on the rocks, no chaser.'" Jack laughed, Sang gave Son a pathetic look, and the waitress just stood there grinning like a Cheshire cat, as if she was thinking how she was gone put herself on ice."

"'Son, you hit on every woman you see.' Sang said as she shook her head. 'Baby, get me a vodka and OJ, and bring the gentlemen shots of OG and beers.' As the waitress was walking away, she hesitated and looked back over her shoulder, to make sure Son was checking out her switching hips. But, to her dismay, what she saw was Son flirting with the cigarette girl. The waitress returned with their drinks in a flash. Sang said, "Damn, baby girl! You workin' it tonight, I aint never seen nobody work fast as you. Son, be sure to give her a big tip."

"The lights dimmed, and the room grew silent enough to hear a mosquito pee. A spot light shone on the stage where the band conductor stood dressed in a white suit, the coat was long with wide lapels and wide padded shoulders. His pegged trousers were high-waisted, wide-legged, and tight cuffed. It was called a Zoot suit. It was designed by (like most things, back-in-the-day) colored men. The conductor, also wore a white pork pie hat with a multi-colored red & white feather. And with a baton in hand, he shouted 'Ladies and gentlemen, it gives me great pleasure to introduce a young new voice out of Philly, Miss Billie Hardaway.'"

"Sang turned and smiled at Jack, and the empty chair where Son was sitting. 'Where the hell is Son?' Knowing full well that he had slipped off with either the waitress, cigarette lady, cheater woman, or God only knows who. 'He aint nothin', but a hoe!' Sang said, as she and Jack laughed."

"So you see that's why I stopped her from filling your head with all her nonsense. She was the first to curse, always had to be right, and loved to fight. You bout pegged her right by calling her Ante Insane, because she had some crazy ways about her. I never told Jack, but I originally named Mary Jane, Mary Jacklyn. I noticed it was not correct at the hospital, but I didn't say anything, especially since she couldn't stand the sight of Jack for her first three months. I'm thinking it was just a mistake, but Sang tells me later on, she changed it from Detroit, passin' as a white woman on the phone. Even after Jack had a conniption about her changing Bernice's name, I knew she wasn't done with her meddlesome ways. That's why when my fifth baby was born, I didn't even bother to name him. I just waited to see what Sang was gone do, and don't you know, when I looked at the birth certificate and saw Nathaniel Lee, I didn't say a word. I did the same thing with the birth of my Sixth child, and she named her Veronica Ann. But I guess when you were born she was really seeking a reaction from us, because she named you twice—Donna Marie and Joe Ann, and then nicknamed you Reba. I don't know if it was the four year gap or if she was just as tired as I was after giving birth to twins, but she allowed Sara to name them Dawn Anthony and Dwan Adrel. I loved her dearly, but she was more than a notion."

8: PASSIN'

"AS SANG LISTENED TO Billie sing, she thought about how they met at the train station in Alabama. Sang stopped at the ladies room before boarding the train. She had to use it so badly that she went into the Whites only bathroom because no one could tell that she wasn't white. Upon entering, she noticed a woman at the sink, feverishly searching through her purse, seemingly distressed. She wanted to ask if she was ok, but didn't want to get exposed. When she finished her business, she went to the sink and washed her hands. A white woman came out of a stall and stood at the sink next to her. But instead of washing her hands, she pulled out her lipstick and commenced to freshen up her makeup.

"Sang thought to herself, 'some women are just nasty.' The lady looked at Sang and said, "I like that suit you're wearing, I'm on my way to California, what about you? Sang smiled, then with a sense of entitlement and proper speech, she said, "thank you, I'm not headed to California." The lady said, "well I never, I was just trying to make conversation." Sang said, "Well I'm not interested in conversing with women who don't wash their hands, after using the facilities." The lady left abruptly. Sang noticed the lady, she saw when she first came into the restroom, was still digging in her purse. Sang also noticed something that white people could not detect as easily, and that was that this woman was a colored lady passin' for white. So Sang looked across the floor of the toilet stalls, to ensure the bathroom was empty, then walked over to the sink next to her and whispered, "Hey sis, is everything ok?"

"The woman smiled nervously, and whispered, 'Hell naw, I cain't find my damn ticket to get on the train.'"

"Where you headed?"

"Back home to Harlem, New York. I came here for my grandma's funeral. I barely could afford to get here and back but I had to come, my granny meant the world to me. I even risked passin' as a white woman just so traveling wouldn't be so damn uncomfortable. She smiled as she lit a cigarette that she had stored in a shiny silver case, and offers one to Sang. She takes a long draw and exhales. "By the way I'm Billie, my friends call me BB."

"I'm Willie." Billie gives her a strange look. "I shit you not sista-girl, and my friends call me Sang." They both laugh at the similarities in their names."

"Well, Sang, where are you headed?"

"Detroit, Michigan."

"Listen, I can buy you a ticket to get back home, and you can pay me back when you get straight."

"What you done did, robbed a bank?"

"Naw! Sang said a little too seriously."

"Calm down, Sang, I was just messin with you." Billie said looking around ensuring the coast was clear. "So, does your nickname mean you can hold a tune?"

"Naw, it mean I can sang my tail off." Sang said, in a matter-of-factly tone.

"Well I don't know if you looked back there, lately, but that would take a whole lot of singing. They both burst into laughter. The bathroom door opened and a white older lady entered and stared at them, as if they were too happy to be white. Silence filled the room, only to be broken by the older lady saying, 'good afternoon, please don't let me interrupt. Enjoy your youth, I can tell that you're single and about to go off on an adventure. I was once young!' She winked and entered into the stall. She continued talking as she pulled, and tugged to free herself from her undergarments. As the old lady continued talking about her youthful adventures, Billie gestured for Sang to follow her, as they tipped out of the bathroom."

"Sang's train to Detroit was scheduled to leave within the next half hour so she suggested they go and buy the ticket to Harlem."

"So do you have a job or something waiting for you in Detroit, Sang?"

"No, I'm on vacation for the time being."

"How long you gone vacation?"

"I don't know, I guess as long as it takes. I guess you could say I'm starting a new life."

"Then you should visit Harlem! You will love it, I can show you around. Girl there is singing and partying like you aint never seen before! Billie was talking fast, like a used car salesman, making an offer that was too good to be true."

"Oh, so you like to sing?" asked Sang.

"Yah, I've been known to carry a tune but maybe you can teach me a thing or two. We can travel the world, Billie & Willie passin through." Billie said as she held her hands in the air, as if she were reading a marquee.

"Sang used the opportunity to get a good look at her new friend. She looked exotic like an Indian princess. She had light bright must be white skin, long thick eyelashes, wavy jet black hair pulled back in a chignon, pearl earrings, and a white Camellia pinned on the right side of her head, slightly above her ear. The flower accentuated a round beauty mark on the inside of her ear. A single strand pearl necklace laid over her silk canary yellow collarless neckline dress, and coordinating three-quarter length sleeve coat, navy blue gloves, hand bag and shoes. Billie was 5'6" with a flat chest, small waist, and narrow hips.

"Sang wanted to take the older lady's advice and be adventurous, but she was being tormented by her Alabama cautious ways. She had to convince herself that it was ok to experience the unknown. She had to remember that God was everywhere, so she would never be alone. And that he gave her the ability to handle herself in uncertain situations. She had to encourage herself, and if it didn't work out, she had enough money to leave."

"Do you see a phone booth around here, I need to call my folks in Detroit and tell them I'm going to New York!"

"Billie screamed with excitement and gave Sang a bear hug. Sang bought two regular passenger tickets, and they boarded the train looking like two adventurous white women on holiday. They were greeted by a porter and directed to their seats. Sang had purchased regular passenger tickets, but they were seated in a private car. The porter winked at B.B., then closed the door. Sang whispered, 'girl I don't know how we ended up in this private car, I bought us regular seats.'

"'That was J.B.'s doing. Replied B.B. That's the porter's name I know him from The Club in Harlem. He plays the Bassist were I hang during jazz sessions.'"

"J.B. stopped by to ask if there was anything he could get them. He spent more time catering to them, than any of the other passengers."

" No, we're good. Can you come sit for a bit? I want to introduce you to my new friend. Willie this is J.B. Gillis, one of the finest Bassist in Harlem. J.B. smiled and bowed, he was a handsome man, and at first glance you would think he was a white man, standing tall and handsome in his blue uniform, but his hair grade didn't make the cut. 'I was just telling Sang about Harlem night clubs and the speakeasies.'"

"I told her we, gone start on 131st and Lenox Avenue at the Savoy where you can see Earl Tucker. He made up this dance called the Snakehips. Billie laughed, while swinging her hips, that boy can move just like a snake. Then we gone slip over to the Savoy Ballroom where they doin the Lindy hop."

"Yeah, you gone like the Savoy it has this long dance floor

and a raised double bandstand," JB chimed in, quietly, while smiling and shaking his head in agreement.

"Then off to 142nd Street to the Cotton Club to check out Cab Callaway's Band."

"HI-DE-HI-DE-HO!" J.B. said, while waving his hands in the air.

"Now, next door is the Radium Club, but we only goes there on Sunday morning around about 4 or 5am for the big breakfast dance."

"Don't forget about Club Hot-Cha!" said, J.B.

"Oh Yah, but I don't hit 7th avenue, til I make my rounds, besides don't nothing jump off till after 2am."

"Right, right. Be sure to ask for Clarence he'll treat you right."

Sang was getting dizzy watching them go back and forth.

"Now between Lenox and 7th ave. we have Connie's Inn, Lafayette Theatre, Theatrical Grill, and Gladys's Clam House," Billie says as she uses her hands to indicate the order.

"Yeah, that Gladys Bentley is really classy. She wears a tuxedo and high hat while she tickle the Ivories," J.B. says with a sincere facial expression.

"And if you want to taste the best fried chicken on the earth we gotta go to Tillies."

"It's gone make you scream!" JB exclaims while rubbing his stomach.

"It's next door to this place called the Log Cabin. Billie said in a slow and alluring voice.

"It's an intimate little spot, you know what I'm sayin." JB said as he winked and blew her a kiss, while tip toeing and looking side to side, as if looking to see that the coast was clear."

"After that we cross over 7th avenue and chill for a bit at Smalls Paradise," said Billie.

"Café Au Lait girls and dancing waiters," J.B. said imitating a dancing waiter.

"Then, Yeah Man is a late spot." Said Billie.

"You goin to Yeah Man? " J.B. asked.

"Yeah Man!" Billie says matter-of-factly and they burst into laughter.

"If all this partyin goin on, how yall eat and pay yall rent?" Sang ask jokingly, but serious.

"We sing for our supper," Billie replied.

"And throw a house party for the rent!" J.B. says finishing her sentence.

By the time they arrived in Harlem, Sang and Billie had shared the details of their lives that they wouldn't tell the average person, but each kept their skeletons securely under lock and key. They were calling themselves "Billie & Willie, best friends and damn near twins." J.B. invited them to come join the jam session on Saturday, it was his day off from the A-Train. Sang was excited, even though she had no idea what a jam session was, but she knew she wanted to be part of it, if it involved music.

9: THE PARTY IS OVER

AFTER A WEEK, OF nonstop partying and covering all the spots Billie and J.B. previewed; shopping; hanging with talented musicians and singers; witnessing drug pushers and addicts. But, what really cooked her cake, was when she realized her new friend and mother where part time singers, and full-time prostitutes. At that point she was well done.

As she awakened in her hotel room, still dressed in the clothes she wore out the night before, she thought about her week in Harlem. It had been a blast, she could even say it had been the best time in her life. But at the end of the day, all she could think about was that her people didn't have nothin' to show for all that talent, other than exhaustion. All those talented colored people were enjoying what they did best, but white folks was still makin all the money. Colored folk were just happy to entertain, as they smiled, danced, and sang along. But they weren't good enough to even enter through the front door. It was just some dressed up slavery.

"She could hear Memaw saying, 'Baby, enough is enough. Learn from the conies, the weak can be stronger, if he use wisdom for guidance.' Then she heard the voice of Grandma Louisa, 'you a fool mix of the worst parts of yoh momma and daddy. When you learn to control that truth, then you will find your way.' Sang kicked off her shoes, pulled the blanket over her head, and went back to sleep."

Billie knocked on Sang's hotel room door to pick her up to go to the Clubs. The time had cycled around to J.B.'s off day again. The plan was to meet with him, and start living for the weekend. Sang yelled, from the bathroom, "Come on in, the door is open."

B.B. entered yelling, "Sis, this aint Alabama, you cain't go round leaving your door unlocked. You inviting trouble in, and he don't refuse no invitations," as she surveyed the room.

"'Well I knew you was on yoh way, Sis'" Sang said as she turned the shower water on. "I'll just be a minute, make yourself a drink.'"

"B.B. immediately spotted Sang's purse peeking from under the bed pillow, she hurried over, opened it, smiled, and took some money out, and tucked it in her brassiere. She returned the purse, exactly as she had found it, then made herself a drink, and sat at the vanity table.

As soon as she sat down, Sang shut-off the shower water. '*Yep, I'm from the south, but I didn't just get my mammy's tit out my mouth,*' Sang thought as she watched her light-fingered friend from the cracked bathroom door. All the while suppressing the desire to just walk out, and kick her in her throat.. But, she immediately calmed down because that was the sole purpose for setting the purse bait. She needed a sign, to determine how much longer she needed to stay in Harlem before trouble found her.

Sang came out of the bathroom dressed in her slip, walked over to her purse and opened it and looked at Billie. She pulled out her cigarettes and said, 'want one?'

"Billie was cool, except for the beads of sweat that had accumulated on her nose, shook her head no."

"Sang lit a cigarette, puffed and exhaled. She then placed the purse back under the pillow, readjusted it, as if she needed to put it back as she had found it. She walked over and made herself a drink, then sat directly across from Billie."

"I've got plans to open a club, and with a voice like yours, we can partner up. That way you won't have to lie, cheat, and steal to make ends meet." Sang wasn't one to mince words and she was still pissed.

BB was busying herself at the vanity table putting on lipstick and patting her hair as if she found a strand out of place.

"'Girl, I do believe I would surely die if I left Harlem." She paused for a moment, titled her head, squinted her eyes, and bit her bottom lip, as if taking a moment to consider the offer, then she said, 'Yeah, I would die from boredom in Michigan.' BB laughed as she made her body convulse, as if she was having an epileptic seizure. 'Baby! This is, who I is. I appreciate you, sis, but B.B. gots to be B.B.! Besides, Detroit can't handle all of this!' BB said, as she stood and smacked her hips. Sang laughed along, but her heart was heavy. BB hugged her tight like a frightened child, as if she wanted to go, but Harlem had her bound and gagged.

"She reached into her bosom and pulled out some money. As she placed it on the bed, she said, 'You know, I never paid you for that ticket, so this should cover it, plus some.'

"'You are good people, lil sis, and I will never forget your kindness.' BB said in a quiet voice as if she didn't want Harlem to know she still had a soul. BB rushed for the door, hesitated with one foot outside, turned and cocked her head to the side, smiled and said, 'lil sis, I'll come sing in your club anytime, just holla.' She kissed her fingers and blew a kiss towards Sang.

'I'll be seeing you soon,' said Sang, as she caught the invisible kiss and placed it on her heart. The door closed and Sang didn't know if she would ever see BB again, but was assured that there meeting was for a reason, and God would reveal it in due season. Sang said a silent prayer for her new friend then checked out of the hotel and took a cab to the train station.

She got back on that train and slept nearly the entire journey to Detroit. Sang was awaken by the train conductor's announcement as he walked through each car, 'Next stop Detroit Michigan, arriving on track number 3. If this is your final destination, please exit from your rear, check your area for your belongings. Sang opened her purse to freshen her lipstick, but it was missing. Sang started laughing, and thought to herself '*that cow done stole my lipstick.*'"

10: THE RIGHT (NOT WHITE) KIND OF WOMAN

"SANG BOUGHT A NEWSPAPER as she made her way out of the station, and sat on a bench waiting for Junior to give her a ride to Cousin Ruthie's house. She began thinking about the stories she heard about Junior. She was just 5 years old when they moved away, so she didn't remember them. She overheard, during a grown folks conversation, that Junior was around 15 years old, when Cousin Ruthie, just up out of nowhere, left to go up North for work.

"They said it was 'to escape from trying times;' however she never quite knew what that meant. When she attempted to ask, Grandma Louisa told her to stop asking questions, and learn to listen. Sometime later, she overheard her telling Jack, 'It had been six months before I heard from Cousin Ruthie, then I received a letter. But I told her not to call or write, just wait a while then send an envelope to the general store addressed to Henry E. Booker. About 6 months later, Mr. Upshaw hands me an envelope addressed to Henry E Booker postmarked from Toronto, Canada. When I got home, I open it and this here newspaper clipping was inside. I see a picture of hundreds of colored folks, three white soldiers, and one white man in a suit and cane, posing in front of a tall brick building. I knew it was from Ruthie, but I wanted to see if I could spot her in the picture. I used that magnifying glass of yours, and I laughed till I cried. Right in the front row of that picture, stood Ruthie and Junior, on either side of one of them soldiers. Knowing Junior, we probably got kin-folk all over Canada. ' Sometime afterwards, I looked at the clipping, and I read the article. It was about these Black Canadians, posing with a Premier in Queens Park, during a dedication ceremony in memory of an all-Black, battalion that served in WWI."

"Is that a true story?" Reba asked her mom.

"Well, after Sang shared the story with me, I asked Jack if it was true. He said his grandma did tell him that story, and showed him a newspaper clipping. He said grandma told him, 'Henry E Booker, was the message letting her know they made it. The words 'here ok' was within the name written on the envelope.' She told him that story about Cousin Ruthie and Junior, after some white girl came by and asked for a ride on his horse. She said Junior had a passion for white girls. His passion caused him and his momma to leave in the middle of the night, like they were some runaway slaves traveling on the Underground Railroad."

"Grandma Louisa said, 'I sent them away, after I had a dream about 5 fish hanging from a tree, and all the fish heads look like Junior. I told Cousin Ruthie, it be best for Junior, if y'all go up North. Junior was a good boy, and he could fix anything he touched. But, he was sickly and couldn't take the heat of the cotton fields. So, Boss-man chose ole Junior to do handy work around his house. He never thought much of him being a threat to his five teenage girls, due to him being a midget. Well unbeknownst to Boss-man, all five of his very tall daughters, ranging in ages from 13-17, found Junior to be cute as a teddy bear. Well, in the one month's time that he worked for Boss-man, all five of them girls was with child. Now, Junior say it wasn't him. But, that must not be what those girls told they daddy. Cuz nine months later, Boss-man was looking to lynch ole Junior, after those 5 girls pushed out 5 lil mulatto baby girls. He called on me to deliver them babies. Two of the sisters gave birth on the same day. I tell you this so you know to choose the right (not white) kind of woman.'

"Jack said if it happened, it was before he was born, and he had only known Cousin Ruthie to live in Detroit." Mary Alice hesitated then said, "'Reba, ask Siri."

'Siri, search the web for Black Canadians picture during a dedication in 1920 at Queens Park in Canada,' Reba said, as she spoke into her iPad.

'Here's what I found,' replied Siri.

From the list of web search results, Reba selected, 'Black Canadians pose with Ontario Premier Ernest Charles Drury….occurred in the 1920s.'

The page opened to an article on Black Canadians and an array of inapplicable pictures. Upon scrolling down the page, she selected the history tab. She saw a picture of Mathieu de Costa, the first recorded black person to set foot in Canada. Further down, she came across Anderson Ruffin Abbott, the first black Canadian to be a licensed physician. She continued scrolling and an article on the Underground Railroad caught her attention. She had forgotten that it was utilized to get thousands of fugitive slaves from Detroit, Michigan to Canada. She continued scrolling, then stopped when she came across a picture of Black Canadians pose with Ontario Premier Ernest Charles Drury at Queens Park, 1920.' She tapped the screen with 3 fingers, to enlarge the photo. There on the first row, on either side of a white officer was a short dark complexion woman and a short dark complexion man, resembling pictures she had seen of her Cousin Ruthie and Junior.

Reba showed the picture to her mother and whispered, "Grandma Louisa was a spy!" Reba and her mom laughed till they cried.

11: JACKSON IVEY

REBA DIDN'T THINK SHE had any questions to ask about her dad. She took every opportunity to ask as many questions as possible—some may say too many—during her youth.

Reba told her mother, "My daddy said he never met a person that he couldn't get to smile, or regretted the camaraderie. He said everybody liked him, except his daddy, Lewis Ivey, Jr. (a.k.a. Huddy). As a result, he was confused during his younger years. He said, his daddy cursed at him so frequently that he was beginning to think his nickname was 'black bastard.' If it were not for their strong resemblance, he would have contributed his daddy's indifference to his mother's infidelity."

"He said, 'I was raised by my Grandma, Louisa, she was my daddy's momma. For the longest time, I thought me and my brother lived with her because Granddaddy died and she needed us to work the farm.' He chuckled. 'Then one day, Grandma said I got on her last nerve, with all my crying, cursing and complaining about how my daddy had no cause not to like me. She said I was getting so bad, and hateful that she felt it was best that I know the truth, 'before it blocked my manhood journey.'"

"She said, 'Baby, your daddy don't hate you, he hate yoh momma.'"

"I was stunned, all I could say was, 'Huh?'

"Yes, you heard me right. When yoh sistah, Sang, was born, yoh momma wouldn't have nothin' to do with that child – wouldn't even nurse the sweet baby. If it were not for Miss Willie Bee, Sang would have perished. Ever since that day, yoh daddy and momma been fighting like two roosters in a hen house. I reckon Pearlie mixed up making babies with baking cakes.' Grandma Louisa chuckled at her own analogy. 'She was thinking her dark chocolate skin when mixed with Huddy's light chocolate skin, could only result in a brown shade of chocolate. That fool taz woman nearly lost her mind, after giving birth to a white chocolate baby. It wasn't till you were born, that Pearlie started acting like she had some damn sense. Course, it was most too late to fix what had gone wrong between them."

She walked over to the sink, and stared out the window as she retold the real story, "As time passed, Huddy became more and more hateful towards all his children, except for Sang. Your older sisters settled for the first man they courted, just to get away from them. On the outside, it didn't seem as though your brother cared, one way or the other, about them and their foolishness. But, I suspect, the rage that shows up when he's fighting, is fueled by all his pressed down anger.

"I'll never forget the time he raised up to Huddy. It was a Friday night, and Pearlie and Huddy got to fighting, now yoh momma could fist fight, as good as any man. They was out in front of their house, raisin' all kinds of sand, cuz they was full of that fire water. Well this particular night, Son, who was only 'bout 12 years old, he rose up and with one punch, knocked Huddy on his back. Pearlie looked down at Huddy laying there on the ground, smiled and staggered into the house. That next day, Pearlie was still mad, and meaner than she was before she passed out. She told Sang not to worry about school no more, cuz she was going to work in the cotton fields. Then, she told

Huddy and Son to get out of her daddy's house. Since you was her baby, you could stay. So your daddy brought you and Son to live with me, and he took Sang with him. And yoh momma & daddy aint never fought, or hardly spoke to one another since. Your daddy stayed on his job, up at Mr. Ivery's horse ranch, sometimes months would pass before he'd come riding on that horse, suited like a bigwig. At first glance, if you didn't just know him, you'd be inclined to think he was Mr. Ivery."

Grandma Louisa smiled, and hugged her grandson. As she held him tight, she said "You know you look just like your Grandpa Lewis. You didn't get a chance to know him, God bless his soul, but you have his beautiful hickory brown skin, and you got ways just like him. Now that was a man, he was always kind, and would help most anybody in need, even though he didn't have much himself. Don't let your daddy mean ways touch your spirit, he loves you, but he's been wounded, and it aint got nothing to do with you. You hear me boy?"

"Yes Ma'am," He replied, as he looked at Grandma with reverence. He thought his grandma knew everything; so if she said it, then it was so. As a result, he never cried, complained, or cursed again about his daddy's contrary ways."

"He told me that Grandma Louisa taught him everything she was taught as a child: sowing and reaping from the earth, respecting nature, and to only kill for food to eat not just because you can kill, using the sun and the stars for direction, how to fist fight, use a knife as a tool or weapon, using a bow and arrow, training and riding a horse bare back. He caught on to everything she taught him, as if it were second nature to him."

"Sometime later, his father told him, he watched him from afar, as he worked the land, and fixed everything that broke around his mother's house. He said, he didn't know how to apologize to him for being angry all those years. It took him close to, two years before he got his life together. He remarried, and started visiting his mother every Sunday afternoon. He had hopes of establishing a relationship with his boys, but as soon as he walked in the door, my dad would say hello and goodbye at the sight of his father, and immediately leave the house before any other words could be spoken. And he was intent on not returning, until his father had vacated the premises. Grandpa Huddy never saw my Uncle Son during his visits. By that time, he had moved in with a lady friend, and was working at Natham's slaughter house."

"Grandma Louisa didn't try to disguise the favoritism she showed towards my daddy. She told her son, 'It's not just because he looks like your daddy, but because of the person he has shown himself to be. I never have to ask him to do his chores, and when Son left, he took on all the chores without complaining. I swear, the only thing that boy has ever complained about is the way you have treated him.

'But don't you worry about that, because I told him the truth. I declare, it was the best thing I could have done for that boy, because he aint cried since. I told him he's a good boy, and that I'm proud of him. But I can't, at this very moment, say the same about you, Mr. Lewis Ivey, Jr.

'I didn't raise you to be carrying-on that way, and me nor did yoh daddy ever treat you so unkindly. Hell, we got the white man for that. Jack don't need no extra damn pain, and the white man certainly don't need no extra help.'

'You right Ma, Lord knows you right. I'm gone do right by my boys, mother, I promise you that.' Huddy replied.

'Well, you know Jack's birthday is in three weeks from this Sunday. He'll be fourteen, and I want you to get him a horse like the one you ride,' Grandma Louisa said without batting an eye.

"He told her, he would do his best, although if it had not been for shame, which was weighing heavily on his shoulders, he would have told her, his horse was not owned by Negroes. It was a special breed, and it had been gifted to him by the owner of the horse ranch, where he worked. But that would have only exposed more of his guilt that he had been feeling for deserting his family, and living a life that his folks would call, a house nigga. He left his mother's house appearing as dignified as when he arrived. He was looking like a perfect target for the BANITs (bad-ashy-negros-in the thicket) that were just up the road, watching and waiting to rob and kill him."

"My daddy had been in his hide-away spot for over two hours waiting for his dad to leave. That's where he retreated, every Sunday, when his dad came over to visit Grandma Louisa. He was resting on the higher branches of a bald cypress tree, that he named 'Chief.' Through the eyes of a child, and with a grandmother that encouraged him to allow his imagination to be his source of entertainment, the tree resembled the upper torso of a strong muscular man with long locks of hair blowing in the wind."

"Before his dad started visiting, he and Grandma Louisa spent their Sunday evenings on the porch, and she would tell him stories that mostly starred Chief. The tree was ferociously anchored about 100 yards in front of the farmhouse, it had a trunk that was 17 feet wide and stood 132 feet high. Grandma Louisa utilized Chief in teaching him about nature, her stories were about a Chief that ruled over all the animals in the forest by studying the behavior of the animals in the woods. She told him, 'quietly sit and watch the animals, they will teach you how to follow your natural senses.' Now, Uncle Son listened, but he was too old and set in his ways to be influenced by his old grandmother's childish stories, but my daddy enjoyed every moment and looked forward to story time."

"He told me, he spent hours in those woods climbing Chief, so much that the squirrels moved to other trees. Numerous hours were consumed inspecting, and interacting with birds, insects, reptiles, and any other creature that crossed his path. Overtime, he became very knowledgeable to the natural and pure order of the animals, but most importantly he had to show them that he was chief over them all. It seemed unnatural to witness the animals not scatter into the woods upon his arrival, as he ran up the long bark and grabbed a branch with both hands and lifted his body onto a branch, and laid facing in the direction of the entrance to their farmhouse.

He used his telescope to get a birds-eye-view of his house, and as far as 3 miles down to the bend in the road.

"He witnessed many unscrupulous acts committed against people traveling down the road to his home. Thanks to his telescope that Grandma Louisa got from the renew section in Mr. Ervin's general store. The time he spent interacting with nature proved useful during hunting season, he returned home with more rabbits for stewing than all the older boys in the hunting group. In spite of the way he treated his dad, he still watched out for him when he came to visit. Because every time he rushed out of the house, when his dad walked in, he retreated to Chief and watched out to make sure the BANITs didn't mistake his dad for a white man, who dared to travel in their neck of the woods. He had seen many unsuspecting white men disappear, traveling up and down that road, sneaking to lay with Negro women whose husbands were working long hard hours in those cotton fields; or Negro women who had no husband, or man to speak of, but had a house full of mulatto babies. The first time his daddy showed up, he realized his fair skin could be the cause of his own undoing, so he met with the BANITS and informed them of his daddy's destination, and they agreed to grant him safe passage. They respected my daddy, but more importantly they knew his brother, Son, if provoked was crazier than them, and wouldn't hesitate to cut each and every one of them. Even so, my daddy remained vigil since he knew that he was dealing with a gang of contrary angry men, and honor amongst the hostile had limitations."

"I guess your daddy did tell you quite a bit, hmm, he never told me about what happen between his momma and daddy. It was a sore subject whenever I asked," Mary Alice replied.

"Did you know, during the day, my daddy also used his telescope to keep a watchful eye on you ma?"

Mary Alice smiled, "Yes, I knew that, but what did he tell you?"

"He said, he watched you when you sat under a weeping willow tree in the back of your house, as you walked your younger brothers down to your daddy's store, and as you loaded your red wagon with your mom's handmade quilts, which you delivered to neighbors in November. He said, that was before he mustered up enough courage to say anything to you, other than a routine hello in passing. He said he liked you, but you wasn't like most of the other girls he knew. You were a smart and pretty girl, your clothes were always crisp and clean, and the way you walked with your head high, always cordial and smiling, and spending your spare time reading books under that tree. My daddy said he was accustom to the girls making the first move, even his brother's girlfriends flirted with him, rubbing his curly hair and hugging him too tight while saying "Son, your lil brother is so cute, I could just eat him up." He even said, one of Uncle Son's girlfriends would always seem to show up when he wasn't home."

"Really, did he say what her name was?" Mary Alice said in a jealous tone.

"Umm, not that I can recall." Reba laughed to herself, thinking a woman never changes. Really? How long ago was that, ma?

"Do you remember when you dropped off a quilt for Grandma Louisa, and my daddy walked you back home?"

"Yes! He told you about that? Mary Alice said in a surprised tone.

"Yep," Reba said confidently. "Grandma Louisa told him, 'Jack, prepare a basket of green beans and a basket of squash for Mary Alice to pick up, she gone deliver us some quilts tomorrow.' He was delighted to oblige her request, because this was his chance to spark up a conversation with you, and maybe even ask you to be his girl. That night he asked if he could take his weekly bath a day early. The next day he presented himself before you bathed, and wearing a clean shirt and overalls. When he saw you pull up he said, 'Hello Mary Alice how are you today?' Reba changed the tone of her voice to impersonate a crooner.

"And you said, 'Hello Jackson Ivey, I'm doing very well, thank you for asking. And how are you this beautiful day?'

Reba said in a soft voice. Mary Alice chuckled as her daughter imitated a scene from her childhood.

"My daddy said you looked like an angel standing there in your white blouse and white skirt."

"He told you that?" Mary Alice asked astonished that her husband remembered what she was wearing, and cared enough, for that segment of their lives, to share it with their daughter.

"Yes. Stop interrupting, I'm in character." Reba smiled realizing her mom was getting a kick out her retelling her daddy's version of their first flirt.

"'I'm feeling great, now that I see you,' he said flirtatiously as he surveyed you from head to toe.

"Well I'm glad I could help," You said with a smile. Then asked, "Is your Grandma home? I came to drop off these quilts that are in my wagon."

"Yeah, I'll take them. And she sending these baskets of vegetables to yoh momma," My daddy replied as he pointed at two of the largest baskets he could find when he prepared them the day before.

It was obvious the baskets were too large for both of them to fit in your wagon, so you said, "well I'll have to send my brothers back for one, because both of those baskets cain't fit in my wagon."

"Hmm, how about I put one in your wagon, and I carry the other one for you," My daddy said that's why he chose the large baskets.

"Ok, if it's no trouble," You replied.

"It's no trouble Mary Alice, I needs to discuss some things with you anyway. Just wait right here while I take these quilts inside to Grandma."

You frowned at him and said "I needs to say hello to your Grandma, it would be disrespectful to do anything less. You are acting mighty peculiar Jack Ivey."

"So y'all went into the house, and Grandma Louisa did exactly what my daddy was trying to avoid. She enjoyed visitors and held them hostage for at least an hour getting the latest news about whatever they had to offer. Y'all sat at the table in the kitchen and had a glass of sweet water while Grandma Louisa talked for what seemed like forever to my daddy. He interjected when she finally took a breath, and said 'Mary Alice need to be getting back home, Grandma.'"

"You rolled your eyes at him, and said, 'No it's ok, I can stay a little longer.' Then you whispered to my daddy "don't disrespect your Grandma.'

My daddy said, that's why my Grandma liked you, because you were very respectful, and not boy crazy. So, he didn't say another word, just sat patiently waiting for Grandma to unloose you. He said, after about another thirty minutes, she gave her closing statement, 'Well baby, thank you so much for stopping by, I certainly enjoyed your company, be sure to tell your momma I said thank you for the quilts. Jack, why don't you walk Mary Alice home?'"

"So, you all were walking down the road talking and laughing, then out of nowhere, you ask the wrong question. 'Why you don't live with momma? I mean, I see your momma all the time, she comes by my house practically every day to see my mom. And she has been looking mighty strange, lately. I only mention it because she seems lonely, or something, and my mom seems pretty upset after talking with her, which usually ends with your momma running out of the house, looking like she gone hurt somebody.'"

"My daddy wasn't expecting that question, and had anybody else asked him that, they would've been picking themselves up off the ground. He hadn't thought about it, or didn't want to think about the day that his momma told them to get out. But, nonetheless, my daddy still loved his momma and visited her often. But grandma said, she was cantankerous and going through the change. He said, at the time, he didn't know what that meant, but what he did know was that his momma had little to no patience, and she was convinced that my daddy had jinxed her. She said, he would set her on fire, then put it out, then light her up again. I also knew, I wasn't gone discuss my living situation with Mary Alice, at least, not on our first date. So, my daddy decided it best to change the subject, before he had to knock you out about his momma." Reba giggled.

"So instead, he asked you, 'I see you sitting in the backyard of your house under the tree, why you sit by yourself while the other kids are playing?'

"He said you got the message, that he didn't want to talk about his mother, and you just answered his question. You told him you loved reading, so every free moment you retreated to that willow tree. You said your brother wrote to you from overseas, and he sent you pictures and books. You said, 'I love reading because for that short period of time, I don't have to be a Negro living in Pittsview. I can imagine myself in another place and time. The more I read, the more I want to travel and see the world. There's a big world out there Jack! A world beyond the United States, a world that doesn't look at you and me as if we don't belong, or have a right to happiness.'"

"My daddy said, he was starting to think he opened a bag full of rattle snakes when he asked you what you was doing under that tree. He said you was just going on and on about reading books, he looked up and you had talked all the way to your front door. He said he wasn't able to get a word in edgewise."

"He shouldn't have asked, besides he was the one who changed the subject." Mary Alice said in her defense.

"He said all he could say was, "Well Mary Alice, it has been a pleasure walking you home, maybe next time we can talk about something other than books.'"

"He said you laughed and said 'I know reading is my passion, my brothers and sisters always telling me I talk too much about books, and absolutely nobody else cared about reading a book as much as I do. But I thank you Mr. Ivey for listening. Would you like some lemon water, and to sit for a spell on the porch swing with me?'"

"My daddy hesitated because he didn't want to hear you talk no more, but then you said. 'And I promise not to talk about the books I've read.'"

"He laughed, then said, Yeah!

"But soon as y'all sat on the swing, here come your brothers and sisters: Willie, Ervin, Linda, Cora, Joseph, Anna, Obie, Daniel and Walter. They were excited to see him, and began talking and laughing until it was time for him to head back down the half mile journey to his house.

"During the walk home, my daddy said he thought about his day and decided even though he didn't get to spend time alone with you, he still enjoyed the time with your sisters and brothers. He imagined you and him getting married, and having lots of children that would enjoy being around one another, just like you and your family.

"After that day, whenever you went to the tree in your backyard to read, you would look toward that big ole tree, in his front yard, and waive."

12: TRIG

"MY DADDY SAID, IT was love at first sight, the morning he awoke to find a colt with a reddish brown upper body, a streak of white streaming down the center of his head, light brown mane and tail, white lower half with specks of brown around his trunk, and the lower part of his legs were white as if the horse were wearing knee high socks. He named the colt, Trig and spent the majority of his spare time with his horse, training him to obey and follow him at command, as if Trig were his pet dog."

"He took Trig for his first appearance at the Juneteenth celebration at the frog pond. Trig was a head-turner and my daddy's brown skin had a reddish tone, tanned by the sun, which gave him the appearance of an apache as he rode bareback through the gathering. He said, he got more than his fair share of attention from the girls that day. But, he was hoping to impress you, since he considered you his girl ever since he walked you home. But, he said you was playing hard to get, and you intentionally didn't look his way as he passed by you. He figured you was jealous of all those girls giving him extra attention because of his horse. But he wasn't thinking about those girls, that's why he made a point of yelling, 'Hey Mary Alice,' as he passed you. He said you was trying to act like you didn't see him. He said, 'everybody saw me because I was with Trig, and Trig was a head turner for every man, woman, and child.'"

"He said, you finally came to your senses and smiled and said, 'Hello Jack, hello Trig. He has grown to be a mighty fine horse, Jack.'"

"He took advantage of another opportunity and asked, 'Maybe I can bring him by your house some evening and take you for a ride.'"

"Maybe, if you ask properly. You said flirtatiously, then changed the subject. 'Will you and Son be playing on the baseball team this year?'"

"Hell yeah, I'm the best pitcher this side of Alabama." He laughed and dismounted Trig like an Olympic equestrian. "Those niggas can't win without the sun and the moon!"

"I couldn't help but laugh, because even though he was acting like he was why cow's mow, what Jack said was partially true. He and Son were the two best players on either team, and always entertained the crowd with their trickery," Mary Alice said smiling at the memory.

"But you had to keep him grounded, huh? Is that why you told him, 'You should be a clown in the circus.'" Reba laughed.

"But my daddy had found his swagger, and grabbed you by the waist and whispered in your ear, 'Well I'm not clowning around when I say I love you, Mary Alice.'" Reba laughed and said, "I know that must've swept you off your feet!"

Mary Alice laughed and said, "You're foolish just like your daddy, but if the story was told in truth, what I said in return was, 'good luck playing ball Jack, and nice seeing you Trig,' completely ignoring his flirtation as I rubbed trigs mane.

13: GRANDMA LOUISA IVEY

AS JACK GREW OLDER, his Grandma Louisa recognized that he also grew wiser. She decided to tell him another story. But this one, was different from her usual life's lessons type. This one was about her.

"She said, 'Jack, the end of my days are drawing near, and I need to tell you something. I aint never told nobody, not even yoh daddy.'"

"'Yes, Grandma what is it?' He asked as he turned towards her to give his full attention."

"I was born in Carolina. My father, and his father were Cherokee Indian. When I was a young girl, my father taught me everything, and that I have passed on to you. Along about the same time that I became a woman, the White man came on our land, and told us that the government was moving all the tribes to a territory out west. My people fought for our land. My father and brother were killed during this war. Many more died, either from the lack of food and water, as we walked for many days, or from the white man's disease that he brought upon us."

"When the chance came about, my mother, Ziyeh, and me

escaped along with some others. We hid in the woods, and mountains where the white man was unfamiliar. We lived off the land, as we always did, but we had to keep moving and we had to split up."

"After many moons and sunrises of traveling, we were resting in the woods and was awaken by the sound of gunfire, and the scattering of animals. We laid still on the ground, as we were already covered in leaves, next to a fallen tree bark. A group of men with rifles, mirroring the various shades of tree barks in the forest, rushed by us. Then one of the bark face men stopped suddenly, and rested on the tree stump where we were laying. He nearly stepped on me, he pulled a rag from his back trouser pocket, removed his hat and wiped the sweat from his brow and neck, he rested for just a short spell, then he swiftly moved on to catch-up with his group.

"'We got up, after his footsteps were out of hearing range. I saw his rag on the ground, near the stump where he had been sitting. I picked it up, and held it to my nose, to learn his scent. This was the first I had seen of men of such color. Ziyeh slapped the rag from my hand, and told me to leave it be. She told me, the bark face meant to leave it, so as to mark his trail, and we needed to be on our way, before he came back. Well, I was sick and tired of running from the pale face, and now we had to look out for the bark faces too. I sat on the ground and refused to run any more. Ziyeh sat beside me, and said nothing. I sat with my eyes closed, and I prayed for deliverance. When I opened my eyes, the bark face man, that had stopped earlier, was standing in front of us, offering water and food. Then he spoke a language I didn't understand. But, I decided he was saying, 'Your God has sent me; eat and drink.' So we ate and we drank. He stepped back and watched us eat. Afterwards, he reached down and picked up his rag, he looked at me and gently smiled. We just stared at him. He spoke some more, and we stared some more. Seemingly disgusted, he walked away. After a few steps, he came back, pointed to the sky, then said something else, and beckoned for us to follow him. We followed him to his home, a small house situated on the edge of three acres of farm land.

"I couldn't understand his words and he couldn't understand mine, but somehow we managed through the rough spots. He seemed capable of looking at me, and just somehow know what I needed. He was very respectful towards me, and Ziyeh. We moved into his one room house and helped with the chores of the land, and he taught me his native tongue. But Ziyeh refused to learn, she said it was the language of a people without a soul. She never spoke a word until we were completely alone, then she would speak in our native tongue.

"By the summer of 1897, I had taken the name of Louisa Ivey, and I gave birth to yoh daddy, Lewis. Then, in 1899, yoh Auntie Etha was born. When we heard the government was sending out a surveyor to each home to account from everybody in the house, I believe that was the Census of 1910. We gave Ziyeh a new name, Violet Allen, and we decided, we would tell them we were Mulattos from Carolina. I was Lewis wife and she was of no relation, just a widower with no other means. You see if the census takers got wind of us being Indians, they would send us to the territory out west. But the Negroes had so many shades of colors resulting from relations with white folk, they couldn't say for sure what race we exactly belonged. By the time the Census taker came to the farm, they assumed Ziyeh had lost her natural mind, because she just stared, as if they weren't even in the room."

"My daddy asked, so Grandma, what's yoh real name?"

"SeeLow," she whispered.

14: HUDDY'S VERSION

"YOH DADDY NEVER DID tell me about his momma, but Huddy told me plenty.

"He told me he laid there on the ground, mad as hell that his son had just knocked him on his back, and madder at himself because he was too drunk to get up to do anything about it. In his drunken stupor, he thought about killing that boy, and his mammy. But, the truth of the matter, he couldn't muster up enough strength to command his body to get out of the middle of the road. Fortunately for Huddy, he had two children (Jack and Sang) that felt empathy toward his condition. They managed to relocate him to the floor inside the house, where he could have time to recover, without risk of being trampled or devoured by an animal.

"The next morning, he awoke to Sang screaming, 'Why do I have to leave school, I'll get a diploma in one more year.

"Her mother took offense to her back talk and said, 'Because I said so, dammit! She shouted so loudly, it gave her a severe migraine, and her neck and ears became so hot, that she actually touched them to see if they were on fire. 'I'm sick of every last one of you light skinned slick bastards, and all y'all need to get the hell up out of my house,' as she pointed at Son, then Sang and ended with Huddy.

"Sang shouted, 'I hate you, you aint my momma.' Now the relationship between those two had not gotten much better, since the day Pearlie rejected her at birth. The peculiar thing was that no one taught her to despise her mother, or even told her that her momma rejected her on sight, but it appeared as though she remembered.

"Huddy gathered up his children—including his dark-skinned son, your daddy—and left as Pearlie had demanded. He said he was inwardly glad to be set free from what he called, 'a sixteen year war.' He said the only thing that kept him at the house was his responsibility for the children. 'When they momma gave me an out, that I had been longing for, I says to myself, I aint never going back!'

"Sang was gathering her things, and screaming, 'I hate her, and I aint never comin back to this damn house,' as she kicked a chair over on her way out the door.

"Even though Huddy was thinking she took the thought right out of his head, he told her, 'don't say that baby girl, that's ugly, and it don't look good on someone as pretty as you,' then he winked at her. She smiled as she always did when her daddy reminded her of her beauty. Huddy held her hand, and Son carried Jack on his shoulders, as they walked the path that led to Grandma Louisa's house.

"Grandma Louisa was willing and able to take them into her home, besides the boys already came over every day. It had long been Son's responsibility to take care of the farm, since it had been many years since Grandpa Lewis and her mother had passed on into glory. She thought the relationship between Huddy and Pearlie was doomed from the day Sang was born. Grandma Louisa had a hard time liking Pearlie after that, but she did what she had to for the sake of her son, and her grandchildren.

"Huddy asked his mother for her help for a while with the boys. He said, 'That fool taz woman has put them out,' he chuckled nervously, 'and me too. But I'm gone go up the way, and see about getting a better job. I'm taking Sang with me, so you won't have to contend with her crazy momma, because Pearlie done came up with some cockamamie idea for Sang to quit school, and start working in the cotton fields.

"Louisa agreed, but she knew her son hadn't just come up with this plan during the walk to her house. She figured he had been planning his escape for a long time, and had already taken up with that mulatto girl, Mellie Ivery. She also knew, it was not by chance that Huddy started working for Abraham Ivery (Mellie Ivery's daddy) at IRS (Ivery Ranch & Stables) the very next day."

15: CALUMENT

MARY ALICE WASN'T INTERESTED in fame nor great fortune, she wanted to experience life as a single woman, then get married, buy a home and a car, raise a family, and give back to her community. She had nearly checked everything off on her bucket list, but she still had more to give. She had lived out her single life in Cincinnati, Ohio; married her childhood sweetheart, Jackson Ivey. They bought their first home, they had nine children, and had been instrumental in bringing eight of her eleven siblings, as well as a multitude of other family members, and friends moving from the south to East Chicago, IN. In fact, the Calument area of East Chicago was populated with all of the folks she knew from Pittsview and Mississippi, with the exception of a few interspersed Polish families.

The residents considered Jack and Mary Alice Ivey as elders of their community. On Sundays, after dinner, she walked with their children around the neighborhood, and stopped along the way to talk to the neighbors about any problems, or concerns they had with living in their community. When problems arose, she promptly contacted the various city officials, with whom she developed a rapport, regarding any matters that involved her neighborhood's resolution. She also counseled new parents concerning marriage and properly raising children, and assisted neighbors in need of help. She had become their unofficial go-to-person. If there was anything going on in Calument, Mary on Kennedy knew about it.

Jack and Mary bought a home on Kennedy Avenue, the first street and the last block in the Calument area. It was an ideal street to raise children. There were Polish Americans and African Americans living side by side on their block, and their children played with one another. During the summer months, they had impromptu block parties that began at dust. Where the children played hide and go seek, under the street lights, while their parents sat on their front steps, or some came with chairs, or some just chose to stand and lean on the fence. Unlike the south, warm months in the north, were only for a short time, so they had to take advantage of this brief time to socialize with their neighbors. The winter months were harsh and spent indoors, only the children fraternized during inclement weather.

Juvenile misconduct was nonexistent on this block of Kennedy, because every elder had the authority to boldly let that child know, his parents would be informed of their wrong doings before he made it home. And every parent made sure their child was accountable for their wrong doings.

"We've lived on Kennedy since 1946, and we've had the same phone number. That's why they call me Mary on Kennedy." Mary Alice said proudly. "Of course, not every street, or every block for that matter, in the Calument was as peaceful. No, that only happens in fairytales. Besides, my people figured, what good is prosperity if you couldn't throw a proper party to celebrate having it? After all, the same partying Pittsview people who came up north, were looking for a frog pond of sorts, where they could socialize after the work was done. As a result, there was a tavern on each of the five streets, three night clubs, three liquor stores, a record shop, three beauty shops, and a barber shop. They didn't work to just party, so there were also, 5 corner stores, one grocery store, and a laundromat. We, the people in the neighborhood, nicknamed the tavern on Kennedy 'The Bucket of Blood.'"

"Why was it called The Bucket of Blood?" Reba asked. "As a child, I was scared to pass the place alone, I took the meaning literally."

"Mm-hmm. That was our intention, with a name like that, you'd have to be dumb, or stupid not to be afraid. We just couldn't tell the children that the eagle flew on Friday and every Saturday night somebody got beat, cut, shot or killed. In those days, your fists were the weapon of choice, but an occasional switchblade or gun was not strictly verboten."

Mary Alice chuckled, softly. "But that wasn't the only thing we had going on that was illegal. We all played the policy. Me and Jack were friends with Money, he was the head colored business man in charge."

"Really? Tell me more!" Reba said, as she slightly leaned forward readying herself to hear the exclusive inside story about the infamous Money P. of EC."

16: MONEY P. OF E.C.

"MONEY LIVED IN A big house secured behind a brick fence with a steel security gate entrance with a guard booth. The local residents called it 'the money project.' It was built in the prairies behind McCook Avenue. Years later, his house was cleared and low income houses were built, and we just called it the projects. Anyway back in the spring of 1951, contractors cleared the land and enclosed it with a 6' brick wall. All we knew was what we read on the contractors sign – no trespassing, Money project. Once the wall was erected, they started laying concrete, built one big house and two smaller houses, planted grass and trees. Once everything was done, next thing we knew, he had moved in."

"Money owned and operated the policy, or numbers game of chance (like the Indiana lottery we have nowadays). He offered short-term loans (like the payday loan stores you see nowadays), bars and neighborhood social clubs with back room gambling (sort of like what we have now on the casino boat). The people in the Calument area gave him the utmost respect, not just because he had six body guards with him at all times. But because he provided our community with lots of jobs for men, women and children. They said he was the richest Negro in Northwest Indiana. But I knew something they didn't know."

"Even Jack was taken in by his kind-heartedness. He said, 'Mary, he seems to be ok, whenever our paths cross, we shake hands, and he says the same thing every time. 'You be show to come see me, Jack, if you ever need anything.' I told yoh daddy, that he really should keep his distance from those kind of people."

"What are 'those kind of people'?" Reba asked, as she raised her hands and formed finger quotes.

"The kind that go to jail. Jack had a job and integrity that he had to uphold. Although, I must give Money his proper respect for not allowing drugs or prostitution into our community. There was no gambling on Sundays before 5pm. They said it was because he was a God fearing man, and I know he was a trustee at our church."

"They said he owned the new preacher, the good Reverend Johnson. Of course, you cain't believe everything they say, because I met Pastor when I lived in Cincinnati, I just never knew his real name. But ever Sunday I would just smile when I looked up and saw ole Heartache delivering the good news. He was Money's first cousin on his momma side. Ole heartbreak could preach, sing, and play the piano; but sometimes he seemed to fight with his fleshly being. Often times he held the congregation hostage, until they emptied their pockets of every cent he thought they had on their person. It got so bad the members started leaving, so Money blessed his cousin with a Cadillac, and a generous salary, and the church membership was preserved."

"I knew another well-kept secret about Money, only known by a select few in the neighborhood, and even the powers that think they be in charge, had no idea. But Money chose to tell me, Lord knows I didn't ask him. But I'll never forget, it all started the first time I hit the numbers, he invited Jack and me to dinner. I played 3-6-7: $.05 straight and $.05 boxed. It fell straight, and I hit for $50.00! I had a strong feeling I was going to win, because my hands had been itching something fierce. I got that number from my dream book, it listed the numbers to play for almost everything or situation. I had to laugh out loud, when I later realized the itching was due to a new laundry detergent I bought because it was on sale."

"That next evening, our Policy man, George, delivered the drawings that showed my winning numbers, and I just smiled and silently said, "Thank you Jesus!" I also noticed another piece of paper wrapped around my winnings, I unfolded the paper and it was handwritten note that read:

Congratulations, Mary on Kennedy, on your winnings, I would like to meet you and Jack. You are cordially invited for dinner at my home on Saturday, 4p.m. sincerely, Money."

"I wondered if Money was up to some kind of skullduggery. I just knew he was going to ask Jack to work for him as a runner because of my big winnings, but he had another thing coming and it was a 'No thank you' because Jack wasn't getting caught up in that racket. He had a job that he had to go to 5-6 days a week, plus 9 children to raise, which equaled no time to be hanging out in those streets, chasing and getting chased by Lord only knows what, in that type of business."

"Nonetheless, I accepted the invitation, because, I'm almost too ashamed to admit it, but I wanted to see the inside of that man's house. Every time I drove down 151st Street, I would try to peek through the bars of that gate that led into the entrance of the Money project. Now, I was having second thoughts about going, because I knew my intensions were decadent, and I could hear my mother saying, *"Mary Alice, care killed the cat."* It was just shameful, that I had allowed those gossiping women at the laundromat to arouse my curiosity, with their far-fetched tales about Money's house."

"The neighborhood laundromat was located on McCook Avenue, it had a picture window that faced toward the west, and provided a framed unobstructed view of a 6ft red brick wall that surrounded the Money project, a table, for folding clothes, was placed in front of this window, that only aided in instigating the circle of gossipers, who had never actually been on the other side of this brick wall. However, the tales were down right entertaining, and made washing and folding clothes a jaunt."

"Lil Bit said, 'I heard he had white slaves serving him.'"

"Sweet, shook her head in agreement as she coughed, then puffed her cigarette, and added in a hoarse voice, 'and he has multiple wives.'"

"I laughed along, but I never commented on any of their tales, but I thought to myself, *you can take my folks out of the country but it's hard to take the country out of my folks.*"

17: DINNER IN THE PROJECTS

"SATURDAY HAD ARRIVED, AND Jack and I were getting ready to go around the corner, through the gates and into the Money project. I had gone to the beauty shop earlier that morning and I chose to wear my favorite black party dress, and pearl necklace. I was putting on my makeup, and the thought of why he invited us was still heavy on my mind. I was trying to guess the reason for the invite, and I suddenly got mad at Jack at the thought of him accepting a job from Money."

"So Jack," I yelled, while standing at the bathroom mirror putting on my red lipstick, "don't you forget, just because we accepted Money's invitation to dinner don't accept no job, you can say, you respectfully decline."

"He didn't answer me, but I could see him sitting in the living room playing with the children "Jack was dressed in his black suit with white crisp starched shirt and black tie, "Jack," I shouted again, "are you listening to me? "

"Yes, Mary Alice I am listening to you, I hear you loud and clear," Jack said in a loud and frustrated tone. "I'm not interested in being no runner for Money, if I was I would have accepted the job when he offered it to me when I was at his house last week!"

"I thought my ears where deceiving me, so I ask myself, '*did he just say he had already been offered a job, and did he just say he was at Money's house?*'"

"The kids were laughing so loudly at Jack clowning around, that I had to scream even louder than before."

"Jack! What did you say? I yelled, as I was rushing through the living room to get to our bedroom."

"Then totally unexpectedly, you, who was sitting in his lap, yelled, "Daddy said he thought he left his mama in a pit.' Jack sprung up out that chair, placed his little human tape recorder on the floor, and came into the bedroom where I was getting dressed."

"Jack why didn't you tell me, you been over to Money's house? The only reason I wanted to go was to see the inside of his house." I said irritably.

"I didn't know it was that important to you, it's just a house." He said in all sincerity because I recognized the dumbfounded look on his face. "But you show looking mighty good, Mary Alice,' he says as he kissed me on the neck."

"Thank you Jack,' I told him, for the compliment and for not being impressed by the grandiose of others."

"As we're leaving, and saying good night to each one of y'all, and warning brother and your cousin, Major not to sneak out the house while we were gone. When we get to you, I says to Jack, 'don't think I didn't understand what this child was trying to say,' and we both burst into laughter and left for our dinner engagement at the big house."

"When we arrived at the guard's booth, just outside of the steel gates. After we told him our name, he checked a list of some sort, then asked us for a picture I.D. He looked at the ID, then at us, back and forth a couple of times, then gave them back. As the gates automatically opened, the security guard directed us to follow a half mile winding road that ended at a round-a-about, where we made a right turn, and there we were, in front of a house that resembled The White House. A tall, dark muscular young man, dressed in black, greeted us as he opened my door, and told Jack to leave the keys in the ignition, he would park the car. We walked to the front double doors, which opened before we had a chance to knock. We walked inside and a dark skinned gentleman stood at attention, he was dressed in a black tuxedo, he was bald on top with white thick hair on the sides cut very low. I think he was from overseas because he spoke like Harry Belafonte or Sidney Poitier."

"'Good afternoon, Sir and Madame,' he gestured to relieve Jack of his hat, 'walk tis way please,' the gentleman said as he led us into the foyer, that proffered two curved stairways which led to the upper level, where en suite bedrooms awaited behind doors 1-5."

"We were escorted through a second set of double doors, located between the two staircases, this lead to a drawing room. Upon entering the room I noted, a black four foot sculpture of a naked African woman, balancing a bowl on her head with one hand, the bowl was filled with a bouquet of gladiolas, jonquils, larkspurs, and Asters; a crystal chandelier reflected off of a glistening pearl porcelain tile floor; a piano and a harp where situated in the center of the room; ten French pavilion high back chairs were dispersed in pairs, irregularly around the room; large portraits of negroes dressed dignified and looking proud and prosperous were displayed on the walls in antique gold frames; white sun filtering sheers with purple velvet drapes hung from ceiling to floor, on either side of six, twelve-feet windows. Outside the window I saw a well-manicured flower garden."

"I thought to myself, *this house don't fit in the Calument. Who are you, Money, and what do you really want from us?*"

"My thoughts were interrupted by a man with processed hair combed back with a short part in the middle, he had light brown flawless skin. He was wearing a tailored to fit black, one button, satin shawl collar dinner jacket, a gray ascot, gray slacks, and gray leather shoes. He extended his well-manicured hand as he walked toward us introducing himself, 'Hello, Mary on Kennedy, I'm Money. Jack, nice to see you again. Thank you for accepting my invitation."'

"'Our pleasure Money, my wife's been itching to see this house since it was built, anyway.'"

"I was totally embarrassed, but after nineteen years of marriage and nine children, I was use to Jack's shenanigans. So I held my hands up, as if I had been caught red handed, and said, 'Guilty as charged.'"

"Money laughed and said, 'Well I'm sure my wife would love to give you a tour. Let me take you to meet her, she's in the dining room.' He beckoned for us to follow, as he led the way. I took that opportunity to pinch the hell out of yoh daddy, as hard as I could, for exposing me like that. I had told him, time and time again, so he knew exactly why he had been pinched. He just laughed, as he held his wounded arm because he was a jokester, and never missed out on an opportunity to get in a good laugh."

"We walked down a long hallway that lead into a huge dining room. There was a Negro woman in a white maid's uniform prepping a ten foot mahogany wood dining table, which seated twelve people, while an attractive dark cocoa skin tone young woman stood talking to her. The woman was thin and about the same height as me, but she appeared taller because she had a short torso and long thin muscular legs, and her hair was pulled up in a puff atop her head. Then I noticed we were wearing the same black dress."

"'Mary Alice this is my beautiful wife Mary Ann,' Money said, as he placed his hand on the back of her shoulder."

"We both said at the same time, 'Nice dress,' and burst into laughter. Not only did we both shop at the Mademoiselle Boutique, but we had similar fashion taste."

"She was very friendly, or happy to see down to earth people, because she blurted out of the blue, in a spoiled and pouting tone, 'this table is set for a large group of stuffy folk. Baby, would it be ok, that is, if it's ok with our guest, if we have dinner in our family dining area, it's a lot friendlier?'"

"'Its fine with me sugar, I just want to eat,' Money said with a wide grin on his face. I also noticed the hard stare the maid shot at Mary Ann after her request."

"We followed them through a pocket door, located on the opposite side of the dining room from where we entered. This room showcased flaming torches surrounding an in-ground pool through patio glass doors. We sat at a 4'X 4' square table covered with a white linen tablecloth. The maid served our choice of fried chicken, steak, mashed potatoes & gravy, macaroni & cheese, green beans, corn and corn bread and yeast rolls; and for dessert there was chocolate or vanilla cake and homemade ice cream."

"During dinner Money talked and Mary Ann smiled, or agreed with him but was basically quiet. He said, 'I know that you've heard various things about how I run my business, but I'll tell you the one thing that is true about me, my real passion is the work I do towards the civil rights movement. I believe we are all responsible for our destiny, and should take positive actions toward making this world a better place for our people. My point in saying this, and the reason I asked you fine people to dinner tonight is that I want you, Mary on Kennedy, to think about running as the precinct committeeman for your district. I will support your campaign financially, but my involvement can't go beyond that, because of the type of business I run. Also, there's a project on the table that involves building a new addition, to address the lack of available houses for sale to our people. I believe you can be very instrumental in assessing the desires of the people, and ensuring that these needs are facilitated. Please give it some thought, and get back with me.'"

"If we are all done with the politics, maybe I can give Mary Alice a tour of the house, while you gentlemen have a cigar," said Mary Ann.

"'That's sounds really good,'" replied Money. "'Come with me Jack, I want you to check out these cigars I got from Cuba.'"

"Well, I'm a pipe man myself, but I'll give it a taste," replied Jack.

"We went in one direction, and the men in the other. After about 45 minutes, we re-joined the men in the drawing room. As they were walking us to the door, Mary Ann asked me if I was going, next weekend, to see Cab Callaway at the Cadillac Club. I told her, 'Yes, I was thinking about it, it's going to be a packed house.' But truthfully, I wasn't paying that much money to be in a place, so crowded, you could barely breathe, and all the good seats would be given to the bigwigs."

"'Well we have these extra tickets, unfortunately I will be out of town,' Mary Ann said, as she handed me an envelope. It had 8 tickets enclosed for a reserved table, front and center stage. 'Perhaps you and some of your friends can use them.'"

"Thank you so much, Mary Ann, that's very kind of you."

"I never, in my wildest dreams, expected that to be the reason Money invited us to dinner. I was honored to take on the task, and would've said yes right there on the spot. But first, I had to discuss it with Jack. On the ride home, I asked him, 'what do you think about me getting into politics?'"

"He said, 'Well Mary Alice, I think you got a triple portion tonight. You got to take a tour of the big house, you been asked to be a politician, and you got tickets to the show. I heard what Money had to say about the position, but I suspect you'll look into it further, and I trust that you will make the right decision. Whatever you decide, will be ok with me.'"

18: WHO CAN I TELL?

"I COULD HARDLY WAIT for eleven-thirty the next morning to arrive, so as I could call Sang. We had become best of friends over the years, but Sang told me, once before when I called her on a Sunday morning at six o'clock. 'Mary Alice I run a night club, and it don't close until 3:00am. If you ever call me before nine o'clock, and aint nobody dead, I'm gone walk from Detroit to Indiana and whop your taz.'"

"I took Sang's remarks as a joke because surely she wasn't going to walk two hundred and sixty three miles, but to error on the side of caution," she chuckled, "I never called before 11:30am on Sundays."

"Good morning, Sang are you up gettin ready for church?"

"'Hell no, what's goin on mini Memaw?' Sang, affectionately called me that in memory of my mother, because as I aged I looked just like my mom."

"Well I wanted to ask your opinion about something. You remember, I told you that Jack and I was invited to Money's house for dinner?"

"'Was that last night?' Sang nonchalantly asked, knowing full well that she had been up since 9am waiting for her to call.

"Yes, and we had a great time, the house is just like

115

something out of the movies. His wife, Mary Ann, gave me a tour of the house and I swear for buttermilk—excuse me Lord for swearing—that woman talks nonstop. I can tell you everything about her because she told me everything but what her kindergarten teacher name was."

"Sang laughed and asked, 'like what, girl?'"

"Like I know she's ten years younger than Money; that she grew-up in Harlem, has a younger sister and a sickly mother. She was a dancer at the Cotton Club before she married Money; she said she wanted to be an actress, but she was told she was too dark to make it in the business, so she do all her acting for Money, exclusively. She don't pass a mirror without stopping to admire herself, and mention how long and beautiful everybody says her legs are. Although, I don't know how anyone would get a chance to say anything to her, because I could never get a word in edge-wise. But, back to what I wanted to ask your opinion on. Money asked me to run for Precinct Committeeman."

"What?" Sang replied loudly, dragging the pronunciation as if she was sounding out the word.

"Yes, and I'm seriously thinking about doing it."

"'Well, you always been smart, Mary Alice. I remember, when we was comin up, every time I saw you, yoh face was in a book. Memaw said you was her special child, and the South wasn't gone hold you back. And everybody in the Calument knows Mary on Kennedy. I think you would be a good politician for your community.'"

"Thanks. Oh yeah, I almost forgot, when we were leaving Money's house, his wife gave us eight tickets, front and center, to see Cab Calloway at the Cadillac! I told you he owns that club, didn't I? Well next weekend, he's playing in Chicago, and doing a set in East Chicago, as a favor to Money. Jack told me he saw Calloway at your club, long before he got so famous."

"'Was that a bribe?'" Sang said jokingly.

"Sang, you know you crazy." I said jokingly, but I had some doubt as to her sanity. "His wife is leaving for a few weeks to go see about her sickly momma. I told you she told me everything about herself."

"I'm tellin you." Sang replies as her sinister thoughts were reeling in a red herring. "Hey, Mary Alice, how the kids doing?" Sang ask, intentionally changing the subject.

"They all doing fine, you know Sarah graduates in June and she's one of the top students in her class. My baby's going down to Bloomington, Indiana to college." She said proudly and matter-of-factly.

"I'm so proud of her. You know what, I haven't seen all my nieces and nephews in a while. I think it's time for Son and me to come for a visit. Save two of those tickets for us." Sang said confidently, as she manipulated her way to East Chicago to see her old friend Money, while his wife was out of town.

"Ok, Sang." I said excited, yet disputably thinking to myself, *"Yeah, right you want to see the kids."*

Sang either didn't care for the tone of my voice or read my mind. She immediately got an attitude, and out of nowhere, she says, "Where is my damn brother? Somewhere working, no doubt, while you on the phone talking long distance, and running up the phone bill.

I looked and frowned at that phone receiver, I could still hear her screaming and just carrying on something terrible. I just slammed the receiver into its cradle, and said, "That child just like her momma, crazy as a Bessie bug."

I wasn't gone let her take away my joy so, I grabbed the broom and started swaying my hips and singing, "Look out Money, Sang's comin to East Chicago."

The End.

But it aint over. Mary Alice very cleverly avoided sharing her side of the family secrets—she still got some 'splanin' to do.

Coming soon—Book #2.

ABOUT THE AUTHOR

Donna Ivey-Bryant is an entrepreneur and author. She is a graduate of Indiana University where she obtained degrees in Business/Accounting and Data Processing and Information Systems.
Upon completing her motherly duties and emptying her nest of three children, she has embraced her passion for writing. Powered by the grace from God; and the encouragement and support of her husband, she is eager to begin another journey.